Secret passions and promises to keep.

Charity Langford has a secret passion. Hormonal changes, as this unaware werewolf comes into heat are making her reckless. She's taken to visiting an adult site to get her rocks off. She has no idea that the pheromones she gives off are a temptation for every rogue wolf in the area hoping to bed and wed a princess.

Half-breed wolf, Lucas Kendal, has promises to keep. To guide Charity into heat. To keep her safe. And to avenge his brother. His feelings, even if he had them, mean nothing. He's a lobo, the strong hand Charity needs to protect her and teach her about sex and who she is, and expendable.

Twice in a Blue Moon

Blue Moon Magic ~ Book 2

Honey Jans

Twice in a Blue Moon
Blue Moon Series ~ Book 2
Copyright © 2007 Honey Jans
ISBN 10 ~ 1-62052-029-X
ISBN 13 ~ 9781620520291
This edition for Amazon and others.

Cover Art by Scott Carpenter,
P and N Graphics, Inc.
Edited by Alicia Dean
Proofreading and Formatting by
Jim and Zetta Author and Publishing Services

Published by Shooting Star Books
www.shootingstarbooks.com

Dedication

I'd like to dedicate this book to my fellow Blue Moon Magic authors: Debi Wilder, Shari Dare, and Lynn Crain.

Chapter 1

Charity Langford rushed back to her office in the Langford and Langford IT department, cheeks flaming. Good heavens! She'd just confirmed that at least one of the Langford sisters was getting laid on a regular basis. But really, catching Chas and Justin making love in the executive washroom was just plain embarrassing, not that they seemed to notice her presence or care, for that matter.

She was the one with issues, according to her older sister. But this breach of conduct was way over the line. Even worse, it forcefully brought home to her the sex she wasn't having. She rolled her eyes at her own pity party, conceding that she was overreacting. But at least she had the good grace to keep her sex life, pure fantasy though it was, private.

No one needed to know how much she'd come to crave her daily visits to Dominion.com, and she sure as shooting wasn't about to share her Cyber Laird, so sexually dominant he could make her come from afar with a few keystrokes, with anyone. Just thinking of him made her body pulse with heat and kicked her senses into sharp focus as she heard her staff gossiping in the other room, and damn if she didn't smell cinnamon rolls in the cafeteria. It was all because of her way too vivid imagination, she knew, but it seemed otherworldly and even scary. Now who was overreacting? She rolled her eyes again.

But wait, hadn't Chastity complained of similar sensory sensations when she and Justin hooked up? And even more potently in Charity's mind, her Laird was able to do it to her wirelessly, turning her into a super geek in the computer lab. A wry smile twisted her lips. The man must pack a whopping load of testosterone to affect her this way.

Passing her sometimes too-nosy staff as their gossip abruptly died down, she tried to downplay the fact that she was aroused. Since the attempted hacking attack to her server two weeks back, her staff had acted far more protectively than she liked, probably on her father's orders. He'd been on edge since she'd hit the hackers with her proprietary fireball program, frying their systems from afar, and they'd struck back at her with empty threats. Consequently, her dad had gone completely overboard and hired a nasty, drop dead sexy guard dog of a PI.

She studiously avoided eye contact with said bodyguard—Lucas A. Kendal, PI extraordinaire, according to her dad—as she attempted to breeze past him. Still, she couldn't resist taking a peek. Longish dark hair that curled around the collar of his black tee shirt, sharp whiskey-brown eyes that didn't miss a thing, and a sexy body made for sin; he made her heart race just looking at him. The calculating gaze the dark-eyed stud ran over her focused on her blush and told her he sensed what she'd seen, and her heated reaction to it.

The corner of his hard mouth quirked up in a heartbreaker's grin that made her wet in ten seconds flat, even as it made her want to deck him. If *screw you* could have been conveyed by a look, she shot it back at him. Unfortunately, her displeasure didn't seem to faze him one little bit, the Alpha male jerk.

He stayed at his post, sprawled in a desk chair across from her private office, where he could keep an eye on her, according to him. *"You're not going to give me the slip, sweetheart. Try it again and pay the penalty,"* he'd warned the first time she'd attempted to get away and he'd caught her in the elevator.

Pressed into a corner as he loomed over her, his body heat making her burn, she'd damned near melted. She hadn't dared to ask what the penalty was. Based on his dominant gaze, she had a pretty good idea it involved her bent over his knee. What a Neanderthal. But she couldn't help creaming as the rock hard proof of his arousal pressed against her. Then he leaned in to sniff her neck, and she fluttered inside as he let out a low, primal growl. When an equally primitive growl poured out of her, it seemed to shock both of them as he drew back to look at her.

Time stood still as he stared at her mouth, and she leaned forward, puckering up for a kiss. The elevator doors dinged open, he backed off with a curse, and she sagged against the railing, all stirred up for nothing. Thank heavens she'd found the link for Dom that night or she might have tried to do something drastic, like knock him to the floor and do him.

Now there he sat, dressed in black jeans that fit him like a second skin, and a black tee shirt defining all his muscled glory in defiance of the company dress code. The work she'd assigned him as a cover sat there completely ignored. He stared at her like he owned her and knew she wasn't wearing underwear. Hellfire, it was a wonder he hadn't followed her into the ladies room to find out. The thought sent quivers through her sex.

Cut it out, she scolded herself, squeezing her thighs together to stop the sensual fluttering down below. It was impossible; the man practically oozed sex appeal. Her lips tingled as she stared at him, focusing on his sultry mouth. What might he taste like? She was dying to find out; maybe nibble his square jaw, and dip her tongue into that cute cleft in his chin. *Down girl, he's here to look after you, not teach you the joys of sex at your old maid age of thirty-two.* His quirked brow told her he guessed the sexual nature of her thoughts.

Cheeks flaming anew, she escaped to her office, quickly shutting the door and locking it. Thank goodness she had her Cyber Laird to dim the flames, and help her refocus. This maddening sexual itch, combined with the series of hacking attacks she'd thwarted, threatened to drive her crazy. Ending the barrage of attacks with her special fireball program had made enemies. The pissed-off hackers sent death threats, prompting her father to hire Kendal, who made her want to knock him to the floor and jump his bones. It was a vicious cycle, one she couldn't seem to break. But maybe at the IT conference in Vegas she could find someone who...

Sighing at her wishful thinking, she peeled off the jacket of her business suit, loving the way her silk blouse felt against her bare skin, and rushed over to her computer, late for a date with her cyber master. She had two hours until she had to leave for her staff's annual weekend getaway to the IT Conference. A weekend far away from her annoying babysitter would be wonderful. Maybe she could actually hook up with a charming stranger in Las Vegas, sow a few wild oats, and get this desire for sex out of her system.

She slipped into her desk chair and reached for her computer's keyboard. Her excitement building, she logged onto Dom.com and looked for his screen name. Yes! He was there. *Wolf.* A thrill went through her. She logged on as *Sugar*, and put on her headset, saying softly, *"I'm here, my laird."*

"Follow me to our private room, Sugar."

She shivered, hearing his sexy rumble; a thick brogue that rushed over her like a warm caress, causing her sex to cream as she imagined what was coming. Sex with a guy wearing a kilt—now that inspired all kinds of kinky possibilities, ones she was dying to explore if ever he'd agree to meet her for real. So far, she'd struck out with him too.

With guilty pleasure, she murmured. *"Yes, my laird."* Maybe it was better this way. She could surrender to her online master, get off, and still maintain an illusion of icy reserve in public.

"How many times did you touch yourself today, Sugar?"

His blunt demand made her hesitate, a blush heating her face. As a redhead, she hated her inability to lie, because her blushes always gave her away. Hell, her laird wouldn't know one way or another. After a tense, weighted moment of self-recrimination, she let out a sigh of surrender.

Here comes the Langford upbringing again...finish what you start and never lie to anyone about anything, period. Sighing, she confessed, *"Six times, my laird."* His chuckle made her squirm in her office chair; she was going to get punished but good; and anticipation made her tingle all over. She thought about the vibrator in her desk drawer. Maybe he'd make her come three times in a row like last time.

"What a naughty girl, not to wait for your master's permission."

His scolding echoed her thoughts. Why couldn't she control herself? It had been so easy two weeks ago, but Kendal's presence had seemed to trip an invisible switch inside her, bringing her wanton sexuality to the surface. *"I'm sorry, sir."* She shivered with delight, getting into the secret fantasy. Thankfully, it was just the two of them and Kendal never need know.

"Did you obey my instructions, Sugar?"

She brushed her bare breasts though her silk blouse, loving the free sensual feeling of forgoing her usual bra and panties. *"Yes, laird, I'm not wearing any underwear."*

He took in a deep breath. *"Good girl. Unbutton your blouse for me, and play with your sexy tits, bad girl."*

She shuddered, a thrill going through her at his explicit words, meant to turn her on, she was sure. *"Yes, my laird."* Her hands quickly flew to do his bidding. She slipped the ivory buttons of her white silk blouse out of their buttonholes until the teasing garment hung open. The air conditioning wafted a cool breeze over her budding nipples, and she shivered with delight. She bit back a whimper as her nipples tightened.

With a sigh of pleasure, she cupped her full breasts and fanned her fingertips over the exquisitely hard peaks, murmuring at the pleasure as she stimulated them again in his direction. He'd practically worn her out in the last week, sending her sex toys, having her try the most shocking things on her sexually awakening body. She pinched her nipples, rolling them. *"I'm playing with them, my laird."*

"Excellent. Imagine it's my big hands touching them, getting your tasty nipples nice and hard for me."

Closing her eyes, she pictured her mystery laird, imagining her soft hands becoming his larger harder ones, his rougher fingertips rolling her stiff nipples firmly, tugging on them. *"My nipples are so very hard for you, laird."*

"Now pinch them for me, Sugar, a small punishment for being late."

She pinched them firmly, whimpering at the erotic feeling that shot through her, making her sex clench.

"Good girl, now spread your legs and touch your pussy. Let me know if it's wet for me."

She sighed in willing surrender, leaning back in her big desk chair, and spread her legs, her hand reaching under her skirt to touch her hot pussy. Her clit was stiff and distended, tingling like a million nerve endings were on fire for him, her pussy quivering and wet... She sobbed...sadly, it was also empty. Damn it, she needed him. Still, she rubbed her clit for him like the good little submissive he was turning her into, moaning uncontrollably. *"I'm very wet, sir."*

"Good. Play with that bad pussy, make it nice and creamy for me, but don't you dare come, Sugar."

She stroked her wet slit, her thumb rubbing her stiff clit as she registered his stern command. Not come...that was impossible, and well he knew it. Still she couldn't hold back a moan as she got nearer to orgasm.

"Imagine it's my hand touching you, my fingers slipping inside your wet pussy, getting you ready to be fucked."

She bit her lip on a shaky breath at the F word, her fingers plunging into her damp sex, with a lewd, wet sound she was sure he detected. His sexy growl confirmed she was right. "Yes, my laird. I'm imagining it's you. When can we meet for real?" she asked, desperate for a taste of the real thing. Heck, for all she knew he could be anyone, maybe some dirty old man. She had to find out. And if he didn't make good on these preliminaries, she was going to explode.

"When I think you're ready, honey, and not before."

She groaned at his brusque rejection, but it didn't stop her hot response to his commands, or her growing need for him.

"Do you like the way it feels when my fingers plunge inside you, filling you?"

She panted, her pussy clenching on her fingers as he spoke. "Oh yes, laird, very much."

"Now stop."

Trembling, on the brink of a huge orgasm, her fingers went still at his command. "Please, sir."

"No. You're being punished for playing with yourself earlier. I'll talk to you tomorrow."

Charity moaned as he disconnected, and tried to stop like he'd commanded. She really did, but there was no way of stopping her impending volcanic eruption of an orgasm. He'd gotten her too used to them, too needy.

Her reckless fingers plunged into her wet pussy, pretending they were her mystery laird's, and she groaned, tightening herself around them, trying to imagine they were his cock. *His cock!* Oh god, it tripped her trigger, and she cried out as her wet sex convulsed and she exploded into orgasm. She was dimly aware of her office door opening as she came like an out of control bitch in heat.

*****

Lucas Kendal stood inside Charity Langford's office doorway, blocking anyone passing by from ogling his beautiful she-wolf mate in the throes of passion. *Oh lord!* His cock surged forward inside his suddenly too-tight jeans, torturing him, but he couldn't look away. Still shaken by the culture shock of being rescued by the Elite, only to have his half-brother Lash killed in the raid, he was still trying to get his bearings. Going around like a randy wolf in heat for the first time wasn't helping him stay in control.

The cyber-sex he'd initiated to get sweet, sexy-as-hell Charity ready for mating with him had backfired big time, consequently he was frustrated, horny as hell, and pissed off in general. But he would not be deterred from bedding her. The problem was keeping his promise to take Lash's place as Charity's mate while not succumbing to her charms. Claiming her was going to be harder than he'd thought, because he wouldn't get to keep her.

That wasn't *all* that was hard, he thought ruefully, stroking his cock's raging shaft through his jeans. Good lord she was killing him. He hadn't been able to resist cornering her in the elevator, getting drunk on her sweet, alluring pheromones as he'd scented her blatantly, sniffing her while pressing his cock against her creamy wetness. It made her gasp and pucker up like she expected him to kiss her, shocking the hell out of him. That's when he'd cursed himself, pulled back. He'd regretted it ever after. Since then she'd eyed him like the animal he was, smart girl.

Didn't matter, he'd do what he had to in order to protect her; teach her about passion, sex, and who she was before she dumped him. He was no more than a stud for hire, after all, and it was his role in life. Hell, he ought to be used to it after the Beta's breeding farm.

After the danger of the blue moon was past for Charity, her father would choose a more suitable husband for her from among the Elites, and Lucas would travel on; ever moving in the shadowy world of the Alphas. His feelings, if he even had any, didn't matter. Still, he couldn't help watching her in the throes of an orgasm he'd initiated, feeling like a needy whelp with his first mate.

Charity's pretty face was flushed with passion, her headset still in place, her eyes shut, as the extended orgasm swept her away. His hunter's gaze focused hungrily on her beautiful bare breasts, the tasty, stiff nipples like ripe red strawberries. How he ached to taste them for real. The sweet sounds of ecstasy pouring from her full red lips was like music to his ears, and would be like catnip to any rogue wolf within a sixty-yard radius. This was no longer about a turf war between Wolfen societies. From the moment he'd met her two weeks ago, this had turned very personal.

What a naughty girl, to disobey him and keep playing with herself. He'd have to spank her for it eventually. He knew she'd love it. She was so exquisitely responsive; it was hard for him to restrain his dominant sexual animal instincts. He itched to take her over his knee in retribution and then make love to her until she couldn't think straight, couldn't deny him.

"Want me to take care of that for you, doll?" he asked, working hard to keep the ancestral broad Scots out of his voice. It wouldn't do for her to guess that he and her laird were one and the same. He watched her big violet eyes pop open.

Lucas smiled as her mouth formed a perfect "O" of shock, but true to her royal status, her dismay soon was replaced by an imperious glare as she stared back at him, her fingers still stroking her wet pussy. He could smell her scent from across the room, and his rod hardened in response, lengthening as her startled, maybe fascinated, gaze watched it happen. Hell, yeah, he had what she needed, but first she'd have to obey him.

"Who gave you a key to my office?" she demanded, pulling her hand out from under her skirt and buttoning her blouse.

He kicked shut the door behind him and held up his bare hands. "Look, doll, no key. The door was unlocked." He didn't bother mentioning that his fully developed skills gave him powers she'd never dreamed of; opening a locked door was dead easy. He'd walk through fire to get to her and keep her safe. She just didn't know it yet.

He closed the distance between them, noting her trembling hands as she finished buttoning her blouse. The lady wasn't as unperturbed as she pretended to be. Good, it suited him to keep her off balance. "We need to talk about this weekend."

"Save your breath, Kendal, I'm going."

"Have it your way," he murmured, focusing on her stiff nipples showing clearly through her silk blouse. "I'll have to go with you."

Noting the direction of his stare, she scowled and swiveled her desk chair so that her back was to him, stood, and put on her blazer. "I'll see you at the airport then."

"It doesn't work that way and you know it. I've arranged transport for us. I'll be here to collect you in half an hour," he said, turning to walk out of the room. For all his sexual experience, he couldn't help feeling like the vulnerable one.

Chapter 2

Lucas stalked towards Charles Langford's office, hard and frustrated as hell. Jacking off didn't help, the past week had taught him that. Charity had the only cure for what ailed him, and he couldn't, by rights, take her until the night of the Blue Moon. At least he'd get the pleasure of bedding her before she rejected him. It might be enough to keep him warm during the cold nights to come. He rolled his eyes at the sappy thought. Romance had nothing to do with this, and he had no business thinking it.

Besides, an Alpha stud like him didn't have a clue as to how to romance her, even if he wanted to. It was something he was loath to admit. With the Betas, who'd held him captive during his formative years, love didn't play a part in mating. Sex was for procreation, and sexual pleasure didn't even come into the equation for the females. This trip to Las Vegas was going to complicate matters even further. First, it would be harder to protect her in a crowd, and secondly, trying to wine and dine her in front of her gaggle of women friends would be excruciating. He'd be trailing after them like a puppy dog, he just knew it. He stepped into Charles Langford's office anteroom and Langford's private secretary, Cordelia Bane, looked up with a frown.

"He's a bit busy now."

"He'll see me."

The woman's brow wrinkled with disapproval. One of Charles Langford's trusted circle of Wolfen employees, she wasn't used to rubbing shoulders with low down mongrel Alphas like him. Wolf society ranged from the Elite, like the more-human Langford Clan, down to the Betas—animalistic and deadly. He was an Alpha from the mixed group, a half-breed straddling both worlds, living in the shadows.

"Very well, I'll buzz you through."

Lucas nodded and shouldered his way into the Langford den leader's inner sanctum. Stopping a moment to take in the sight of Charles Langford seated behind his large mahogany desk, Lucas recalled his sire's words.

*"Once you're at their heart, boy, you'll have them where
we want them. That's the time to strike. Never forget, their
superior attitude makes them vulnerable."*

Rowan Angus, the Beta leader, had done everything to
turn his bastard son into a carbon copy of himself; pitting him
against his half-brother Kill to make him stronger and meaner,
more deadly. Having the females of the Beta ply him with sex
as he came of age kept him horny and distracted. The most
powerful tool in Rowan's arsenal, however, was teaching him
to use his dark Beta Magical Powers. They were seductive,
empowering for a youth. To travel through time and space on
just a thought, to walk through any locked door. Still, after
years of what he'd seen as abandonment by the Elite, a
rational part of him saw the brainwashing for what it was—a
cruel power play.

When Lucas had suddenly grew too powerful for Rowan's
comfort, he'd been banished to the mating barns, held
prisoner, his powers bound, to beget the next generation of
bastards. He'd been about to escape with Lash and another
captive Alpha male when the Elite came to save him. They
needed Lash as a mate for Charity, and who were they to turn
down such a generous offer? But things went disastrously
wrong and as he held Lash, mortally wounded, in his arms,
he'd promised to keep their word, to come back and take his
brother's place as Charity's temporary mate.

He gazed at Charles Langford, still surprised that the Elite
leader had seemingly welcomed him into the fold as Charity's
mate. Of course, he knew it wouldn't last. The old man had
needed a wartime Lobo, a stud, to protect his daughter, to
bring her into heat and sexually initiate her, and he fit the bill.
The Elite leader used him just as surely as Rowan had used
him. But this time he didn't mind. He had promises to keep.

The walls behind the Elite's leader were darkly paneled,
the bar in the corner glistened with crystal decanters of good
booze. It was everything an Elite wolf's den should be and
nothing like Rowan's primitive keep deep inside the Brey
forest's gloom. There were no manacles chained to the walls to
hold hapless victims.

Pulling his attention back to the present, he refocused on the Elite leader. Langford looked up at that moment, spearing him with a direct glance guaranteed to make young pups piss their pants. Lucas inclined his head in greeting.

"Well?" Langford asked.

The old wolf said it all in one impatient word, and though they were at cross-purposes, he sympathized with the elder's exasperation. "We leave in half an hour."

Putting down his pen, Langford cracked a smile, sweeping him with a considering glance. "You couldn't talk her out of it, after all?"

"Not bloody likely."

"Yes, my middle child does tend to be a bit headstrong."

"More like too blasted stubborn for her own good." He tensed, recalling her feisty response when he'd scolded her for frying the Beta's hacker's computers. Rowan was no doubt madder than hell and even more determined to worm his way inside these walls. If he had his way, the crazy bastard would die trying. "Frying the Beta's computers with her fireball, especially without corporate approval, was a gutsy move."

Charles's smile faded. "Gutsy yes, wise no. You know her response will only embolden his attacks."

Lucas merely inclined his head in agreement. "She's set off alarm bells inside Rowan's keep, no doubt."

Charles sighed, leaning back in his chair. "After Chastity and Justin's wedding, old conflicts had actually started to be resolved between the clans."

"With one exception," Lucas filled in, recalling how furious Rowan and Kill were when they learned Chastity had married and mated, slipping out of their oily grasps. It was when they'd set their sights on Charity that he and Lash had hatched their plan to get away and warn her.

"I'm afraid so, your sire is as..."

Lucas winced, hating the fact that he was even sired by the mad Beta Leader. "Crazy as ever," he filled in grimly.

"Crazy as a fox," Charles agreed. "Now my dear daughter's stirred up a hornet's nest and brought herself under their scrutiny." Charles sighed. "Her rash behavior is the main reason I agreed to let you take Lash's place as her mate. She'll need a strong hand to protect her and see her through the mating ritual."

Lucas agreed with the headstrong part, but the mention of Lash sent a flicker of rage though him. His desire for revenge still ran hot, but it would have to wait. It didn't escape him that Charles made no mention of the binding. They both knew this was only temporary. Mating ritual, yes, binding, hell no, but he'd known that all along. "Don't worry, I'll keep my word and look after Charity."

"I didn't doubt it for a minute. Maybe it's for the best that you two go to Las Vegas and leave here for a while," Charles said with a nod. "It'll throw her would-be suitors off the track."

Suitors! It was too mild a word. The Beta and Alpha wolves tracking her would be a bunch of sex starved beasts hoping to bed and wed a princess. Bedding could be a fierce and sometimes deadly experience for an untried female, especially one who'd been sexually repressed and kept in the dark as to her identity.

*****

Charity picked up her laptop, just the thing to keep up her sessions with her laird in Vegas, and to keep her from putting the moves on Kendal. She had five minutes before the brooding hunk came to drag her off to the airport. A tap on her door made her frown. Think of the devil, and there he was, impatient as always. "Keep your pants on, guard dog, I'm almost ready."

Her door opened, and her sister, Clarity, popped her head in. "It's not Kendal, sis. We need to talk."

"I can't stop to chat, Clari. He'll be waiting for me."

Clarity opened the door wider and walked into the office. "This won't take long." She handed Charity a small paper bag. "I wanted to give you this new tisane I made for you."

Charity took it warily, trying not to wrinkle her nose and hurt her sister's feelings. Clari was always concocting herbal blends for her to try. Between the noxious brews and her dire predictions, which, thank goodness, hardly ever came true, it made her a pain in the butt at times. But Clari did everything with love in her heart and the best intentions, so she smiled. "What is it this time, another love charm? I told you they don't work on me."

"It's not a love charm," Clari said with a gentle roll of her eyes, adding softly, "You don't need one anymore. It's just some herbal tea to help you sleep."

Don't need one anymore. Her little sister didn't know how wrong she was. Charity was aching to find a real man to love her. Oh lord, did Clari know about her laird, or even worse, her yen for Lucas Kendal? She'd just die if she did, but Clari's open smile made her relax.

Charity opened the bag and took an appreciative sniff to distract her, and a feeling of well-being swept through her at the heady scent relaxing her. "Hmm, Chamomile and mint and something else. You got it right this time. This actually smells delicious. Thanks, sis." She tucked it into her bag and then looked up. Clari still stood there, but now she looked tense, worried. Oh heck, was there another dire premonition coming? She really didn't want to hear it, but she couldn't bring herself to be rude. "Was there something else you wanted?"

"Yes, please be careful, Chari. Dark forces are at work."

Her sister didn't know the half of it. Dark forces indeed. With her crazed hormones toward her cyber laird and Kendal, she didn't know if she was coming or going. And then, as if her thought brought him to her, Kendal was there, filling the doorway behind Clari. "I know all about dark forces." She looked past her sister to frown at Kendal. "He's right behind you."

"It's not Kendal, although..."

Charity stood and walked past her sister, not wanting to hear the reasons for not getting involved with the man. She already knew them by heart, and she was afraid it wasn't going to stop her from trying.

*****

Charity took her seat inside the first class section of the jet. The chill of the leather seat made her gasp, vividly reminded her that she still wasn't wearing panties. Damn, in all the rushing around to get ready, she'd forgotten about being nude below her clothes. A furtive glance at the knowing smile on Lucas Kendal's handsome face told her he'd noticed. Her laird had a lot to answer for.

Her staff was seated back in coach where she usually flew. But no, that wouldn't do for a control freak like Kendal. He'd bumped her up to the first class section where he could *"personally keep an eye on her."* She frowned as he stretched out in the roomy leather seat beside her. Being shadowed by the hunk was getting to her, and for what? He'd already rejected her in the elevator. She stifled a groan at the depressing thought as she sat back stiffly in her seat.

"Comfy?" he asked.

No, she was aroused, and suddenly wet again, damn the man. And somehow he knew it. She heard him take a deep breath and realized he was sniffing her again...*oh god,* her sex quivered. It was so primal, but it was a fact, and it turned her on like crazy. She swept a speculative glance over him, drinking in his potent male presence. Maybe he meant to isolate her here, but he was just as hemmed in by her. Had he done it on purpose?

His slight accent, European maybe, intrigued her anew. It always seemed to get thicker the closer they got, and now it was apparent with his *"Comfy?"* There was something sexy, so reminiscent of her laird, but she knew she had to be imagining it. Wishful thinking again, she decided, but he was definitely prime oat-sowing material just the same. Maybe he could initiate her into the mile high club, she thought with a wry twist of her lips.

Scorching, illicit images of them closeted in the bathroom doing shockingly intimate things to each other played across her mind, making her blush. She shuddered, sagging back into her seat, thanking her lucky stars that Kendal was too busy scanning the fellow passengers with a forbidding look to notice. Boy, she didn't even have the power to flirt with him.

Just then the "fasten seat belt" light dinged, the jet engines started, and she forgot all about flirting. A frightened flyer at best, take offs and landings always scared her, and she realized in a startled heartbeat her stimulated hormones only made it worse. *Oh no!* She squeezed her eyes shut and gripped both armrests, not caring that she was being an armrest hog.

Kendal's big warm hand closed over hers as they took off. His strength seeped into her, and she remembered to breathe again. Thrown back in her seat as they gained altitude, she managed to open her eyes and look at him with gratitude. Gratefulness soon turned to wonder as she met his focused, sexual gaze. He was watching her with blatant lust. Her sex creamed, her nipples tingled and rubbed against her silk blouse.

She couldn't believe it, it seemed she'd actually succeeded in flirting. Now if he'd just make the next move and kiss her, she'd melt all over the hunky PI. Lost in fantasy land, she couldn't help picturing him kissing her, his big warm hand closing over her thigh, sliding up her skirt, touching...

"It's going to be okay, doll," he said softly, rubbing her leg. "I'll take care of all your needs."

She'd just bet he could. She stared at his sultry mouth, shuddering as his warm hand rubbed her thigh. And then he frowned a moment before he let out a growl, thrilling the hell out of her, and leaned forward to capture her mouth. She cried out with excitement, kissing him back, opening her mouth for him when he nipped her pursed lower lip. She let out a yelp and he licked the small hurt before surging inside, claiming her mouth with his tongue.

She whimpered, sucking on his mastering tongue, and moaned in protest when he withdrew, leaving her feeling stunned and bereft. Charity opened her suddenly heavy eyelids, drugged by lust. Why the blazes had he stopped? The flight attendant cleared her throat to get their attention. Good grief, she hadn't even noticed.

"Want anything, love?" Kendal asked her.

Yeah, she wanted a lot of things, mostly him, but it seemed he'd been just playing with her. She simply shook her head, unable to speak because of the lump in her throat.

He looked at her, cursed under his breath, and then abruptly turned to the flight attendant. "We're good."

Charity swallowed back tears when Lucas Kendal flashed her yet another dark look as the attendant moved away. Was that it, he'd tasted her and didn't like it? Or maybe he'd been trying to soothe her flying fears and gotten swamped by her needy response. Either prospect was totally demoralizing. Shit, she had to escape.

She started to rise, and his scowl made her sink back down into her seat. His eyes never leaving hers, he stood and opened the overhead hatch to pull out a blanket. What the hell, was he trying to tell her something? Like go to sleep and stop pawing me. Well hell!

He unfolded the blanket and sat back down, saying, "You look cold, love."

Fury rushed through her. *Cold!* She was red hot and he knew it. But his blatant stare at her stiff nipples poking at her blazer made her even hotter. His burning gaze was like a caress, and she whimpered under her breath as her nipples tingled, jutting out for him, rubbing sensually against her white silk blouse. His smile invited her to look down to see that her top button had come undone along with her reserve, revealing the dusky tips of her breasts through the silk. Hellfire, why had she picked white?

"Pretty," he said. Smiling he reached out to stroke her tingling nipples with his fingertips, brushing them as he leaned over to spread the blanket over her.

She swallowed a moan as he deliberately did it again, tempting her, teasing her as she arched off the seat. "What are you doing to me, Kendal?" she whispered as he frowned, making her subside back into her seat. She sank down with a huff, and then he smiled, reaching out to brush his rough fingertips over them again, a little harder this time.

"Only what you want me to, doll, and it's Lucas," he said after a moment. "Never forget that in this relationship, you hold the strings. Now be a good girl and sit on your hands while I play with your sexy tits."

A blush rocketed through her at his dirty talk, but it only made her more aroused as she did his bidding and tucked her trembling hands under her hips. The restraint of not being able to touch him plus the hot look in his eyes as she complied with his sensual demand almost made her cum as her sex clenched hard. "Okay," she said in a shaky breath that shocked her.

With a growl, he leaned over to kiss her. His mouth slanted over hers. He nipped at her lower lip, and she opened her mouth again to give his tongue access. Charity thrilled at that small possession, his tongue mating with hers before she sucked on his.

She swallowed his groan at her impulsive action and trembled when his hot hands slipped under the blanket to toy with her nipples through her blouse, pinching them, plucking at them, making her squirm in her seat. Totally immobilized by his strong hands on her shuddering breasts, and her hands tucked under her quickly heated bottom, all she could do was feel.

"Why aren't you wearing a bra, love?" he whispered against her ear.

"My laird said..." She drifted off, feeling his fascinated stare as if her words meant more to him than they should. Then his brow quirked in question, and she sighed. Hell, this was another case of her reading more into this than she should.

"Your what?"

Oh god, why had she just blurted out his name. They'd agreed to keep their sessions private. The hard assed too-handsome-for-her-virtue PI was to blame for her loose lips. "Never mind," she said dismissively, trying to shrink back. His eyes darkened as he deliberately pinched her nipples, making her gasp and regaining her total focus in a whimper.

"That's better." He smiled rolling her nubs between his fingers, tugging on them.

She moaned, she couldn't help it as he toyed with her tingling nipples and she felt it down below, in her embarrassingly wet sex. Gads, at least he didn't know how turned on she was. But he was watching her, seemingly studying her reactions to his touch. Stifling a whimper when he pinched her peaks, rolling them between his big fingers, she squirmed in her seat, but didn't reach out to touch him. Her restraint seemed to please him.

"Good girl," he praised.

She fluttered inside at his warm tone. Then went completely still when he flashed her a wicked smile as his hand drifted down her quivering tummy to hover above her mound. Their eyes met, and she nodded, and he lifted up her skirt to cup her wet heat in his hand. *Oh gads, now he knew how out of control horny she was!* There was no hiding her wetness, and she could even smell a hint of her arousal. He seemed to think the same thing as he took a deep breath, and a growl issued low in his throat.

Whimpering, she felt herself melt against his hand and he smiled, slipping a long, hard finger between the lips of her labia. She bit back a cry as starved nerve endings flared to life and lifted her bottom off the seat, seeking more friction. It turned her on like crazy, making her squirm.

"Sit still." He gave her a firm look and pushed her back into her seat with a teasing flick of her clit.

She shuddered as he thumped her clit again, and she whimpered pressing back into her seat. His pleased look told her he read her surrender loud and clear as he rubbed her clit with teasing circles and she trembled.

"No panties either," he commented with a wicked grin. "What a naughty girl. I'm going to have to spank you for that. Don't you agree?"

She moaned, his sensual threat only serving to turn her on more, and his hot words sounding just like her laird's. That's right, if she were naughty, he'd just have to spank her like her laird had always threatened to, and then make love to her thoroughly. His blunt fingers plunged into her wet sex, making her gasp as his thumb pressed on her clit.

She tensed like he'd lit off a bomb inside her, her clit on fire, her sex rippling on him. Oh god, she was going to come, and she saw the wonder in his eyes as he watched her. Her hips flicked off the seat as the ripples started, and she cast him a plaintive look. She couldn't...in public. He pressed her clit hard, and she bit back a moan. He was going to make her. She surrendered, clamping down on his big fingers and he growled, kissing her, swallowing her cry. He rubbed her clit again and again draining every shuddering ripple from her before lifting his mouth.

She collapsed back against her seat, throbbing with after-spasms as he pulled away. Totally stunned, she stared back at him, seeing his satisfied male expression. She'd never had an orgasm that strong, or lengthy, not even with her vibrator and her laird's urging. Lucas Kendal truly had magic hands. Seeing her glistening moisture on his blunt-tipped fingers, she bit back an embarrassed groan.

Then he looked at her, as if daring her to look away, and put them into his hot mouth, sucking her cream off as if savoring it. It was as if he'd like nothing better than to stick his tongue into her swollen sex, to lap up her honey and make her come again. It made her blush, her sex instantly tingling back to life, and she didn't look away.

Instead, her fascinated gaze swept over her surprise lover. Lucas Kendal—who would have thought it would happen. His black tee shirt showed every ripple of his hard muscles as he shifted in his seat as if she made him nervous. His flat nipples were rigid under his shirt, and she itched to reach out and touch them, find out if they were as sensitive as hers were. But damn it, she was still sitting on her hands like a fool, she realized, pulling them out from under her.

He merely gave her a look that said he'd take her to task for it later. Let him. Her fascinated gaze swept down his powerful body to his swollen manhood, clearly delineated by his tight black jeans. The man had a serious liking for black, she thought with mirth as she took him in. And he was huge. She gulped, her fingertips heating as she casually reached out to stroke him, measure him even. His growl, this time weighted with warning, made her flash a worried look up at him.

Beads of sweat stood out on his brow, and a tinge of red colored his face, as if he was struggling to hold back. His manhood leapt under her fingers, and she gasped, pulling them back, knowing she was torturing him even though she hadn't meant to. His whiskey brown eyes glowed with amber fire, she gasped as she seemed to fall under their compelling spell. At that moment, she would have done anything to soothe him. Covering him with the blanket and touching him sounded good, taking him into the lavatory and sucking him off sounded even better.

Her pulsed skittered at the thought, but she licked her lips in anticipation anyway, shocked. She'd never thought she'd want to do that, but something about him made her want to eat him up. Unbidden, a little growl poured out of her throat. *Cut it out.* He was hurting, and she had to help him. "Umm... Do you want to go in the bathroom and we can take care of that?"

His wry glance made her blush.

"Why, doll," he scoffed, "Are you volunteering to take care of it for me? You ever satisfy a man before?"

The insulting question, and the snarky way he said it, broke through her arousal. He clearly didn't think she had what it took to bring him off, or the guts to carry it out. And she had to agree that maybe she hadn't as her confidence waned. She saw it in an instant. He thought she was the boss's rich bitch daughter, playing with him, her daddy's wealth giving her anything she wanted.

He didn't know how wrong he was. She and her sisters had been raised to be independent, to take care of themselves even though they were surrounded by family love. Well, making love to her wasn't part of his job description, and if he didn't want her, she sure as shooting didn't want him. "That's none of your damned business, Kendal," she said, putting on her earphones to shut him out. His stiffening told her he didn't like her rejection, and she froze, half expecting him to do something about it.

Instead, he just tucked the blanket around her shivering body and let it drop as he turned away. She let out a pained sigh at his rejection. It was better this way. The stud wouldn't even be with her if not for his job, and she didn't need his sexual favors. It would be way smarter to have someone else initiate her in the bedroom.

Chapter 3

Lucas trailed Charity and her co-workers from The Flamingo Hotel's IT Conference check-in desk to their meeting rooms, walking through a sea of smiling, chatting computer nerds. But his sexy Charity didn't remind him of any nerd he knew. *His Charity* he snorted in self-derision. He'd truly screwed up on the plane, and now she wouldn't even glance his way. But damn, the way she melted under his touch, licking her lip as she looked down at his hard-on, clearly thinking about sucking him off, still had the power to make him shake. He'd almost come in his pants, losing focus, knowing it wasn't professional.

So yeah, he'd said something crude to distract her, and damn it all, to find out if she really knew how to suck cock. *Jealous much?* She'd responded like he'd stomped hard on her romantic fantasies with his size-fourteen biker boots. Crap! He followed her, his hungry eyes watching her chatting a little too brightly with her staff, totally ignoring him, trying to pretend he didn't exist. He could tell he was being rejected, having been shunned most of his life.

How the hell was he supposed to make up for his gaff? After the incident, she'd done nothing but backpedal away from him as fast as she could go. Still, her sexual response gave him hope and something to build on. Waves of her pheromones—mostly pissed off, but layered with arousal—rolled off her, clear to any wolf on the prowl. The image of her sweet, hot pussy clamping down on his fingers made him growl under his breath, and he saw her blush. Yeah, they were in tune in ways she didn't even understand yet, and it made him want her all the more.

He prowled after her, telling himself a cautious wolf knew the value of retreat, to attack again when the odds were better. His cock straining to get at her wasn't listening. Too bad, he wasn't a cautious wolf when he was around her, but it couldn't be helped. She let out a dismissive sniff, and he tried not to take her dismissal personally, but his blue balls would not be appeased by positive thoughts.

The conference's late afternoon session would give him time to woo her again, to set things right and prove to her that he was a gent. From what Justin had told him, all he needed to do was pull out her chair, get her a drink, be solicitous, and above all, non-threatening. That was the way to get this courtship back on track.

His sharp gaze swept the casino, alert for any signs of trouble. The scents of other wolves in the vicinity hit him in violent waves; Alphas farther off, Betas nearby. Damn, he'd been afraid of this. Rowan already had trackers out for her. He scanned the room, looking for them, but didn't see the hunting pack. Not reassured, he knew that didn't mean a thing.

If he could smell them, they could scent Charity and him. They'd be wary, sneaky, and deadly if anyone got in their way. Shit, Charity's whole staff were Elite Wolves, unbeknownst to her, and she wouldn't thank him for letting them die to protect her.

Damn it to hell. Charles Langford should have listened to him and cancelled the trip. Now he had to devise a strategy to keep *his sweet, sexy Charity* and the rest of her people who despised him alive. He wouldn't be this soft when he was in charge of Charity. A wry smile curved his lips. Tough talk when the untried female in question already had the power to unman him.

He closed his eyes for a moment, summoning all his Dark Beta Powers to mask her scent. The effort had him shaking like a leaf. Those damned mating barns of his sire's had taken more of his strength than he'd care to admit. What Rowan didn't know was that he had the power to withhold his seed from his semen, refusing to beget any more bastards, and at the same time give receptive females pleasure. It had been his only defense at the time as his other powers were bound.

What would Charity think about him fucking all comers as a form of protest? She'd probably curse him as a slavering animal, which he had to admit that he was, deep down. Still, slavering animal or not, he'd protect her with his last breath. Recovering his strength, he ruthlessly pushed away the weakness and covered her, relentlessly satisfied that her alluring scent was covered for the moment.

She stood with her friends waiting for the elevator as he caught up to her, and he realized that she was watching him with concern in her big, violet eyes. Oh hell, some of his internal weakness must be showing, he decided sourly as she looked at his tight expression. It touched him more than he wanted it to as he stared back at her. Since when had anyone, other than Lash, cared about him?

She stepped away from her friends, her fluttering hand reaching up to touch his arm. "Are you okay, Mr. Kendal?"

He burned where her soft hand rubbed his bare forearm and froze in response. The concern coupled with her tender touch affected him more than he'd care to admit, but she was back to calling him Mr. Kendal. "I'm fine, Miss Langford," he bit out, letting her know how it felt and winced when she withdrew physically and emotionally, dropping her hand. He hadn't meant to come across so brusquely, but he couldn't take it back now.

Waves of dislike buffeted him as he felt her staff glowering at him en masse. It was the same hostile wolf society shit he was used to, but this wasn't sticks and stones clan warfare had to come to an end, this was serious. Charity was in trouble and her pack of Elites didn't seem to know. Some Elites, how did they ever survive?

He looked past Charity to Valerie Combs, blonde, petite, and usually bubbly, scowling back at him with disapproval, and Clay Perkins, fresh out of college and devoted to Charity, growled. Lucas lifted a brow, impressed; he didn't think the young whelp had it in him. They didn't like him, but then most of the Elite Clan, with the exception of his cousin Justin, wouldn't give him the time of day. He sidled up closer to Valerie and Clay, whispering, "Betas."

"Oh my god," she said, sniffing the air, giving him an alarmed glance.

"Right," Clay said, standing more erect.

Satisfied that they now recognized the warning for what it was, he turned to focus on Charity. She was glancing between him and Valerie with an uneasy look in her eyes. It hit him like a delightful stroke of her hot little hand. She was actually jealous...of him. He was so stunned by her reaction he couldn't speak for a moment. Shit, to him, Valerie was an annoying, flirtatious kid. The pert blonde couldn't hold a candle to Charity's womanly charms in his eyes, and from her blush as he met her stare straight on, he knew she read it in his eyes.

Good! He reached out to cup Charity's soft cheek, coming between her and her now silent staff. "Something's come up, doll, a little matter I have to investigate. I'm sure Valerie and Clay will stay with you until I return," he said, seeing Clay nod out of the corner of his eye.

"That's really not necessary," Charity protested.

"We've got her back," Clay said.

Lucas slanted them a considering gaze. Instead of looking at him in disgust as the unworthy lobo stud sent to lead Charity down the primrose path to the bedroom, they were looking at him with newfound respect. He gulped, not knowing how to respond as they turned to him for leadership. "Good!" He looked back at Charity, his warm gaze on her hand clutching his arm.

"What's wrong?"

Shit. She was so smart he could never hope to completely pull the wool over her eyes. But he had to try to buy some time while he called for backup and did his best to put down the Betas hunting her. He could read it in her eyes that she was going to try to help him. His gut chilled at the danger she'd blunder into if he let her. "Nothing's wrong."

"Yeah right," she said, letting him go, her eyes narrowing on her staff. "Fine, don't tell me. I'll find out on my own."

"Like hell you will." Lucas grabbed her by the forearm and shoved her into the elevator. At her darkening expression as her staff dutifully filled into the elevator, he sighed. Okay, a half-truth might save his ass from her wrath. "We think the hackers are in the casino," he confided, seeing her eyes widen with surprise.

"Really?" she asked. "You're not just saying that to get me to back off?"

"Really," he said, hearing her staff murmur in agreement.

"In that case, I can help you identify..."

He reached in to punch her floor's button, ignoring her offer to help. That's all he needed—her in the middle of a turf war. She was glaring at him. Pissed off he could take, her in jeopardy, he couldn't, he decided as he watched the elevator doors close on her scowling face. "I'll see you later, doll."

"Don't bother," she snapped. "I don't need or want a damned hard-ass PI babysitter guard dog."

The pain of her rejection hit him like she'd stuck a knife in his gut.

*****

Charity sat stiffly at the table where she and her staff were having dinner that evening, picking at her food as they watched her like a bunch of overprotective hawks. What the hell had Kendal said to them to make them stick to her like glue? *Hackers my ass!* He was obviously up to something. His *"I'll see you later, sugar"* still haunted her. He obviously hadn't meant it, having stayed away all day. Of course her *"Don't bother, I don't need a hard-ass PI babysitter guard dog like you"* might have had something to do with it. She let out a demoralized sigh.

Whatever the reason, Lucas Kendal had vanished, hadn't made an appearance all day. Through the long sessions, the luncheon, even the coffee breaks all surrounded by her dutiful staff, she'd waited for his return hoping for a glimpse of him. God she really had it bad for a hired stud who didn't want her—so much for his promise to see her later. It was about as believable as his feigned disinterest in Valerie after she'd caught him whispering sweet nothings in the gorgeous blonde's ear this morning.

She glanced at the pretty, younger woman, blonde, blue-eyed, and eminently datable, trying not to feel jealous. Who could blame him for wanting her? Every man Valerie met seemed to fall at her feet, why should Kendal be any different? She let out a sigh, having never had that sexually desirable experience herself; except for her cyber laird, she conceded. And then there was the earthshaking one-sided make out session on the plane with Lucas. Hell, he never even let her have a chance to really touch him, even though he'd been hard for her. It was what made his defection hurt even more.

No doubt he was regretting starting something he had no intention of finishing. That's why he was hiding out. His hacker warning was so much nonsense, a bluff so she wouldn't guess his real reason for avoiding her. Lucas Kendal was distancing himself from her, or worse. He might have even called her father and quit. As she thought it, she rejected the notion. He was too dedicated to his job to resign. More likely he was watching her remotely, afraid she'd come on to him again like the awkward virgin she was. His rejection stung, and she blinked back the tear that came to her eyes before they could fall. Fine, she didn't need him. She just wasn't the kind of woman men fell for, and it was high time she accepted that fact.

"I'm turning in," she said, rising to see her whole staff pop up like marionettes. Damn, this was Kendal's doing, and she wouldn't put up with it one more second. "Sit," she scolded, giving them her boss frown, glad to see most of them cave. Only Clay and Valerie remained standing.

"Are you sure you don't want to go clubbing with us?" Valerie urged, pinning her with an alarmed look.

"Yeah, um, sweetie," Clay said with a flush. "It's going to be hot."

Sweetie! She tried not to roll her eyes at the gangly, fresh out of college, younger man's awkward attempt to flirt with her. Kendal must have him running scared to make him do this. She sighed, trying to come up with a way to regain control of the situation, and fast.

Acting as a den mother for her younger staff members sounded about as appealing as watching paint dry. Peace, quiet, and some time to think about her aberrant sexual behavior on the plane were all she needed now.

"No thanks, Clay, I'm tired. But if it makes you feel better, you can walk me all the way to the elevator," she said sourly, thinking of Kendal shoving her into the lift with all the charm of a raging wolf. She gave her staff a look to silence their grumbles.

Clay yawned and stepped toward her, a determined look in his eye. "You know, I'm pretty tired too. Must be jet lag I guess. I think I'll join you."

Charity tried not to roll her eyes at the young man's bad acting. Why was he so determined to stick to her side? He was trying to do as Kendal had said, but there was something more. He had a crush on her; she realized as she met his admiring gaze. Stunned, she didn't know how to react and at the same time didn't want to hurt his feelings. But there was no way on earth she could respond the way he seemed to want.

When he took her arm, she came up with her plan on the spot. She allowed him to whisk her away toward the elevators and then stopped, turning to frown at him. "You can go back with your friends now. My car is almost here."

"I don't know. I'm not supposed to..."

So he was doing this on orders from Kendal not to let her out of his sight. Her ire kicked up, even as she smiled at him. "It's okay. I've got a conference call with my father and you can't be there." She ducked into the car and pushed the CLOSE DOOR button before he could react.

Instead of punching in her floor number, she hit the button for the casino floor. If there was ever a time she needed a distraction to get her head on straight, it was now. She winced, recalling Clay's troubled expression. She was going to have some explaining to do if Kendal caught her, but she knew with his departure that probability was practically nil, damn the man. It was past time to get on with her plan to find some prime oat-sowing material.

Charity looked over her shoulder guiltily, even though she had nothing to be guilty about, seeing nothing but potted palms and clanging slot machines. The tension she'd been carrying started to ease when she walked into the noisy fray and a gray-haired lady whooped with delight as her slot machine beeped.

This was what she needed to relax. She sighed, knowing all she really wanted to do was get properly laid by Lucas Kendal. Never going to happen. Squeezing her legs together, she did her best to tamp down the blaze just thinking about him started. As if her hormonal high was evident, more than one interested male gaze followed her, causing her to blush. For a woman who'd lived a previously sexless life before Lucas Kendal, it was both exhilarating and a little scary.

She flicked a nervous glance at a man with coal dark hair and spooky light blue eyes, who stared boldly at her from across the room. Dressed all in black from his seemingly homespun shirt to what looked like leather pants, he stood out menacingly from the tourists like a wolf among sheep. His interest was palpable, carnal, making the hair stir on her nape and her breath catch in her throat.

Whoa! Him, she didn't want any part of. Her lack of interest didn't seem to faze him. He and two other men fell into step behind her as she turned to hurry away. Charity picked up her speed, her heart racing, feeling cornered despite the crowd.

The threesome carried a predatory air that scared the hell out of her, seeming to move in tandem as a group. At least that's what it looked like to her, but she wasn't about to stick around to find out. She flat out ran, knowing instinctively that she was being tracked by experts. Weaving around a cocktail waitress, she made a fast turn, veering around some penny slot machines, ducked toward the back of the snack bar, and hid behind a potted palm.

Peeking out, she saw the three men standing still together about fifteen feet away, talking in low tones, practically vibrating with fury as their sharp eyes scanned the crowd. Her nose wrinkled when a funky scent wafted her way from their general direction; sweat, grime, and some kind of sour male musk that turned her stomach.

Oh lord they might be the rogue hackers Kendal had warned her about. Maybe she should have heeded his warning and not given her staff the slip. They were after her; she felt it with every fiber of her being. Damn! Kendal would have her hide for disobeying him.

The taller man in the front of the pack made a gesture that caused the other two men to veer off in opposite directions. She gasped. One of them would pass right by her.

A big, strong hand clasped over her mouth, muffling her scream as she was jerked against a muscular body. Panic made her hyperventilate against his palm, until his scent relaxed her. Lucas Kendal! His body heat, sandalwood cologne, and butterscotch breath were unmistakable and like warm, soothing honey against her frayed nerves.

She glanced down at his black leather jacket, wondering what it was about black that men were drawn to. She sank back into his body, sighing with pleasure when the hard ridge of his cock pressed against her bottom. Yum! She couldn't resist giving his palm a little taste with her tongue, making him hiss and let her go like she'd burned him.

"Damn, it's Kill," he whispered, frowning at her pursuers.

Kill? She followed his glance to the leader of the pack of hackers, tall, deadly, spooky eyes, and his name was *Kill*. What kind of idiot called himself that? One she didn't want to meet. She shuddered, registering that he knew the guy's name.

She opened her mouth to ask Kendal about him, and her guard dog frowned, letting out a shushing sound. She clammed up, figuring she owed him at least that. After all, she wouldn't have been chased if she'd listened to Kendal, and his extreme focus said that he was working and was not to be disturbed. She turned her head to frown at Kill, too, wondering why Kendal was so shaken by the sight of him. If it came down to a man-on-man fight, she knew Kendal was the stronger of the two, but she didn't want it to come down to that. The thought that Lucas might get hurt made her tug on his arm, trying to get him to back away.

"Easy, doll," he whispered.

Telling herself the pet name meant nothing, she tugged harder. The man was just doing his job, but her father paid his salary, and she would not be ignored. A growl from the direction of her pursuers halted her frantic attempts to get him to budge, snagging her attention. From the safety of Lucas's protection, she watched the shorter men walk back to Kill, who stopped to sniff the air. Lucas stiffened against her, then plucked the clip out of her hair, letting it tumble around her shoulders. Her eyes widened when he tossed it on a passing waiter's tray as he headed back to the kitchens. What the hell had he done that for? But in a moment, when the pack scurried off in that direction, she smiled at Lucas. How he'd realized that would derail them, she didn't know, but she was grateful.

She heaved a sigh of relief, sagging against Lucas. His strong arms surrounded her, making her feel safe. She couldn't help leaning into him, indulging herself by snuggling against him. Their clinch on the plane came back to her in a heated rush, and she peered up at him through her lashes. As if he could read her mind, Lucas gently set her apart from him. She couldn't help feeling rejected yet again.

"I thought you left," she said, turning to look at him.

"Why'd you think that?"

The confusion on his face was surprising. For a supposedly observant PI, he hadn't picked up on any of her troubled feelings, her feelings of abandonment. Men! "You've made yourself scarce since we landed. Seeing that you've been my shadow since you took this job, I jumped to the logical conclusion that I'd probably scared you off."

He arched a brow and grinned. "Really?"

She didn't like his amused tone one bit, this was serious damn it, and there was more than her crazy, mixed up hormones involved. She was already halfway in love with him. Oh hell, she could teach classes on projection and wishful thinking. It was time to set things right. "Yes, really. I realize that I acted out of control on the airplane. I apologize for putting you in an awkward position. It was the tension of the flight and I misinterpreted your efforts to soothe me." She looked away. "I set you free from your obligation."

"Wow... that was quite a mouthful, doll. You must have been stewing about this for quite a while."

She glared up at him, stung. "This isn't a joke."

"You bet it's not." He stared down at her. "You haven't seen an awkward position, but you will when we get to some of the more adventurous ones in bed."

Charity's jaw dropped as she digested his words, felt the impact of his direct gaze. He hadn't tried to run away, to abandon her. She felt like smiling even though they were in trouble.

"Shut your mouth, doll. Let's make tracks away from those wolves."

Chapter 4

Charity ran to keep pace with Lucas's ground-eating stride as he towed her in the opposite direction from her pursuers. *Awkward bedroom positions*, her mind boggled at the possibilities, but it was of paramount importance that they put space between them and the three-pack who'd been chasing her. Lucas was right to call them wolves, they certainly had sexual conquest on their mind, but she had no desire for group sex. A one-on-one with Lucas would do for her first time, thank you very much.

Her hand clung tightly to his as she sprinted at his side. She had no doubt that Lucas could take care of them, if push came to shove. Even knowing that, she didn't want him to get hurt. "Thanks for coming to my rescue." She panted for breath when they skidded to a halt in front of the elevators and Lucas pushed the up button.

"You're welcome, doll. Be more careful next time."

That got her back up, and she tried to pull her hand from his, but he wouldn't let go. "If you think I go around encouraging things like that, you're mistaken."

"It's not entirely your fault." He tugged her inside the car. "You radiate sexuality. But there are big bad wolves about, and you need a protector."

The elevator doors whooshed closed, and Lucas turned to look at her with a ravenous gleam in his eye. There was a new ferocity about him that exuded through the close confines of the elevator car. The funny thing was that she felt caught up in the same adrenaline rush, but she knew it had nothing to do with the bozos chasing them. Lucas Kendal's very presence made her tingle in all the right places. All she could think about was doing him, now. Her lips burned, her nipples budded tight, and her pussy grew wet as she tracked him across the car. "Did you mean what you said?"

"I know the value of the truth, doll."

"Good," she said with a smile. "I want you to make love to me, Lucas."

He brushed a quick kiss across her lips and stepped back. "You're not ready for that step yet. Besides, I've got my job to do."

Not ready for that step, she was practically panting for him. "And you're doing it very well," she said, humoring the Alpha workaholic. But there was no way on earth she'd let him tune her out. She reached out to place a hand on his chest to feel his heart thudding under her palm. He drew back, going rigid at her touch, and she knew his tension wasn't because of the threat the hackers posed. It was sexual tension, she could feel it in her bones.

He was just as turned on, and she gloried in the knowledge, shoving fear of the rogue hackers away from her consciousness. A glance down at the growing bulge in Lucas's pants confirmed her theory. Still in warrior mode, he evidently was determined to rise above his desire for her and fight.

She growled under her breath, acknowledging that she was becoming just as primitive as he was. What was it about guys and combat that drew their focus? It wasn't like the stinky three-pack who'd followed her were much of a threat anymore. Lucas's muscles rippled with tension as she deliberately stroked her way down his hard body to boldly cup his hard-on and make him refocus on her.

He let out a groan, slanting an assessing glance down at her before giving in and pressing his shaft against her palm. She almost whimpered at the exquisite feeling but knew she couldn't go soft on him now. She had to be strong to get him into her bed.

"God, Charity." He growled, rubbing against her hand. "You play hard ball, don't you."

"I do when I know what I want." She rubbed her fingers down his shaft, measuring him again in her head. He roused, growing harder, longer, and hotter than a blast furnace under her suddenly burning fingertips. "That's not all that's hard," she said with a smile, sensing victory when he groaned even though he shot her a dark look. If he thought she was stopping now, he had another think coming.

There was no way she'd give him, and what promised to be the most exciting night of her life, up. Decision made, she went on tiptoe to capture his hard mouth with her trembling lips. He went stiff as a board, as if fighting both of them, and she wanted to cry with disappointment and almost let him go. Then he growled, jerking her into his arm so that he held her hand tight against his hard shaft.

She relaxed when he kissed her back, hard and deep, his tongue surging into her mouth to master hers in a way that made her cream. Sex fluttering madly, she sucked on his tongue, loving the way it made him groan. His shaft jumped under her fingers.

Charity whimpered when his big hands stroked down her back, stopping to cup her ass and squeeze, and then pull her harder against him. She couldn't stop a little laugh from escaping, and he growled again. His mouth moved onto her neck, hotly sucking and stinging, marking her until she thought she'd swoon. Her whole body was on fire. When the elevator doors dinged open, he backed her out of the car, stopping to press the buttons for all the other floors.

"What are you doing?" she asked, intrigued.

"Throwing them off track, I hope."

The extra precaution made her realize he was still worried and still focused primarily on the job. Damn he had a one track mind. He was taking this a lot more seriously than she was now that she knew she had him for protection.

"Why bother? We lost them back in the casino when you tossed my hair clip onto the tray heading back to the kitchen." She wrinkled her brow at the memory. "What are they doing, following my biometrics in some new way?" If that was true, they were state of the art hackers, not mere thugs like she'd assumed.

He arched his brow in surprise. "You really are sharp as a tack. They're tracking your scent in a manner as old as time, and far more reliable than all your newfangled scientific computerized methods."

So he didn't like computers, he wouldn't be the first. She couldn't hold it against him. *Tracking her scent*...there was something animalistic in it that made her shiver. But it fit in with the stinky pack after her, and, she decided with insight, the sexy man currently trying to derail the elevators controls. Heck, he sniffed her all the time.

"So these are the rogue hackers my dad was so concerned about," she said, seeking clarification. He gave her a duh look that really pissed her off.

"What do you think?"

She frowned back at him, irritated once more by the way he sidestepped her question with one of his own. Was it against his weird PI masculine code to answer a direct question? But his hard look said she wasn't going to break him of the bad habit tonight. It was all the fault of those hackers. Well, there was no way she'd let the stinky jerks ruin this. "I think that they're the bastards who sent me dead roses tied up in a pretty plaid bow along with death threats. If it was cannoli and a dead fish wrapped in a bulletproof vest, I'd say they were sending me a Sicilian message. Oh god, do you think they're part of the mob?"

"It's not that kind of mob," he said with a smile.

Charity heated up as his hand touched her back, and he ushered her down the hall to her room. "Then they were after..."

"You, doll."

Strange men had never come out of the woodwork to pursue her before. But then she'd never been forced to use her fireball program to fry anyone else's system before. Hackers were usually cowardly opportunists easily scared off. These jerks were something else entirely, and by Lucas's grim expression, he was prepared to do anything to protect her from them. She gave him her heart then and there, not caring if it was smart. "I understand. And I trust you to look after me." She gazed at his suddenly amazed expression as he used her key card to open her door.

"I won't let you down," he said. "I'm going to go patrol the halls to make sure they're gone. Don't open the door for anyone but me."

So, he was determined to go play soldier, or maybe he was getting cold feet. But looking at the erection straining against his fly and the hot look in his eyes, she knew that it was duty making him leave. She sidled closer, not wanting or willing to let him go, not when she was so close to paradise.

"What are you doing, Charity?" He eyed her with suspicion as she closed in on him.

"Seducing you, of course." She backed him against a door, going up on tiptoes to pull him down for another kiss. Feeling a shudder go through him, she melted against him an instant before he pushed her away, breaking their kiss. The fevered stare he pinned her with made her quiver, but she would not back away.

"Be patient, Charity, you're not ready for this step yet."

Not ready for this step yet! Good golly he was talking about steps again. Apparently he had a game plan for seducing her and he didn't want to be rushed. Well, the hell with that. There had to be a way to change his mind.

"You know nothing about me, Lucas Kendal. I'm plenty ready for this." At his doubtful look she blurted out, "You happen to be seduced by a woman of experience." She knew the instant he bought her fib when his eyes darkened with displeasure and something else, jealousy. Oh my heavens he was jealous over her. She couldn't believe it when something wildly primitive blazed to life in his dark eyes, making her tremble.

He kicked the door shut.

Charity heard the lock click shut and shuddered with desire and a little bit of fear. Had she pushed him too far? There was a wildly primitive glint in his eye that made her back away, her heart racing and her sex on fire. And why did it feel like she was about to cheat on her laird? Their relationship wasn't real, she reminded herself, trying to push away her guilt. Instead of feeling guilty, she ought to be grateful to him. After all, he was the one who'd prepared her for this, giving her the tools to seduce Lucas Kendal. As if he could sense her mind on another, Lucas bent to kiss her, driving her laird from her mind.

Kissing him back, she lost herself in the present. Her legs bumped up against the bed. She hadn't even realized they were still moving. Time seemed to stand still whenever she was in Lucas's arms. He jerked down the zipper on her skirt, pushing it off her hips in a brisk move that had her naked from the waist down in seconds flat. Hell, it was almost like he and her laird had coordinated this to keep her bare naked down below. Crazy thought, but she couldn't stop it as her hands dropped to cup and cover her mound.

When he arched a brow at her telling action, as if saying that she wasn't ready for this, she bristled, moving her hands away. She wouldn't have him thinking she was scared of this, of him.

"Take off the blazer," he said.

He was daring her, expecting her to fail. She met his gaze with a defiant look, shrugging off her blazer, well aware that her jutting nipples were showing through her white silk blouse. His hot gaze focused on them and she trembled as they lengthened and tingled for him. Well, heck, he didn't even have to touch her to turn her on.

"The blouse next," he said in a gruff tone.

She shivered at his huskily voiced command showing her he wasn't as unaffected as he pretended. Good! Emboldened by the realization, she slowly unbuttoned her blouse, her eyes locked with his. The heat she saw there made her sizzle and burn as she slipped off the garment. Bare to him, she started to shiver, but the admiration in his warm gaze gave her courage.

Feeling brave, she brazenly reached for his shirt buttons. "You're wearing way too many clothes, Kendal." He sucked in a deep breath at her touch and pushed her hands away, and she felt rejected all over again. But the look in his eyes was anything but cold. It was like her touch was painful to him. She winced when she saw his erection practically jump under his fly. Maybe it was. He confirmed it when he pinned her with a "don't you dare move" look and peeled off his tee shirt.

She let out a shocked little gasp. Her fascinated gaze took in his powerful body. His washboard abs she could bounce a quarter off were breathtaking. But they paled in comparison to his powerful V-shaped body all sprinkled with sexy body hair that swirled around his navel and lower, below his jeans. She gulped, teasing, "Lucas, what a hairy beast you are." The sudden flicker of pain in his dark eyes shocked her before he shuttered his expression.

"You're offended."

The grimly voiced words spoke volumes. He thought she was slumming, that she probably wouldn't think him good enough, but he was so wrong. She smiled and stepped up to him, trying to ease his mind and show him how turned on she was. She shuddered when she rubbed her achingly hard nipples against his soft pelt, and he let out a growl. "No, I'm not offended, far from it as a matter of fact. Can't you tell how turned on I am by you, Lucas?" He seemed to relax at her words, and his eyes darkened as he unzipped his fly.

Charity gulped, gazing at him as he shoved down his jeans. The first thing she noticed was that he wasn't wearing underwear either; the second thing was that he was huge. His manhood seemed to fall right into her hand. Charity's palm encircled his pulsing, heavily veined shaft, barely containing it, the ruddy mushroom-shaped head swelling as she watched. She couldn't help but wonder if she could handle it, or him. He was scary big, but she wanted him so much she'd make it work.

"You hold all the strings," he assured her, rocking gently into her hand as he bent to cup her cheek and kiss her tenderly.

His tongue flicked against hers, teasing, tempting, turning her into a melty marshmallow as she moaned, kissing him back, her hand tightening on his thrusting cock. Charity moaned again as her world spun crazily, and she suddenly found herself sprawled on the bed with Lucas coming down on top of her, although she'd been unaware of moving again. This whole time standing still in his arms was a bit disconcerting, but as he pressed her into the mattress, she surrendered to it, just like she surrendered to Lucas. She gazed up at him, trying to memorize everything about him, put him in her mind castle to keep. The heated look in his eyes said she didn't have time to delay. She had a man to seduce before she chickened out, and if he said she wasn't ready one more time, she'd clobber him. He seemed to read her thoughts as his eyes darkened, and he bent to capture her mouth while he dragged his hard cock against her body.

She spread her legs, rubbing her thigh against his hot shaft teasingly, loving the way it made him jerk. His warning growl said she better not be playing with him as his big hand cupped and shaped her breast, and she whimpered and arched into his hand. He plucked at her nipple, stretching it, making it ache with pleasure as she squirmed with need. She tried to rush him, tried to urge him to hurry up, but he chuckled against her mouth and pressed one of his big legs over hers, binding her to the bed, restraining her movements. She groaned with frustration, trying to throw him off so she could move, but he slowly bent to suck her nipple into his mouth hard, and she screamed with delight. She felt the pull all the way to her clenching pussy, and if he didn't make good on his sensual promises soon, she was going to kill him.

Then his hand drifted slowly down toward her sex, and she held her breath, quivering with anticipation. Instead, he tickled her belly button. She growled with displeasure, making him laugh. "Damn it all, Kendal, if you're going to just tease me—"

His hand cupped her mound, pressing against her clit, and she shrieked. "It's Lucas, Charity, say my name if you want to get fucked."

She shuddered at the hot demand and met his heated gaze, not looking away, sensing this was important to him. He didn't want this to be casual, anonymous sex, and neither did she. "Lucas, please..." she cried out as he cupped her heat and squeezed.

"That's better."

She moved to stroke him, and he jumped as if she'd hurt him.

"Keep that up and this is over. Reach up and grab the headboard."

Shaking with need, she did as he said and clutched the headboard, the position opening her, pushing her breasts up for him. His eyes darkened and he bent to feast, sucking one nipple and tweaking the other, and she cried out, shuddering. He was killing her. She groaned and then his fingers parted her labia, stroking the lips, and she whimpered, pushing against his maddening, teasing hands. He smiled and pressed her clit, and her eyes rolled back in her head as she cried out.

"Sweet," he praised, doing it again.

She shuddered and then his finger thrust into her, and she lifted her ass off the mattress. His frown made her settle back down as her sex gripped him hard. He muttered a curse in a language she didn't understand and moved to settle between her legs, his cock butting up against her pussy. She quivered, closing her eyes in bliss, rubbing herself against the hot, velvety head, past caring if he'd object to her moving.

"Look at me, Charity."

Her eyes popped open at his gruff demand and the fiercely hot look in his eyes took her breath away. This was a hell of a lot more to him than a casual lay, and she gloried in it.

"You hold the strings. Do you want me?" he asked tensely.

His body went rigid as he froze, holding back. It was as if he was ready to pull back at the least provocation. Her heart almost stopped at the realization. How could such an Alpha male be so unsure of himself when it came to her? Still gripping the damned headboard, her only move was to rock her wet sex against the head of his cock, making him swear. "I want you, please, Lucas, don't make me wait." It seemed to settle something inside him, and she could swear she saw gratitude in his eyes a moment before he arrowed his cock into her with a fierce thrust. She stiffened, crying out in pain. She'd known it would sting, but this fully stretched feeling was eye watering. He went still, his jaw tightening as he glared down at her.

"Why you little liar," he said, shaking his head. "I can't believe I fucking fell for it. You were a virgin."

She tensed. He didn't have to sound so mad, so cheated. But she had kind of fibbed to him. "I'm not a virgin anymore, thanks to you."

He groaned, dropping his head down to touch hers, and he closed his eyes. "What have I done?"

She burned as only their foreheads and genitals touched. It was like he was pinning her with his pulsing manhood, making her sex twitch and ripple around the invader. She let out a little gasp of surprised pleasure as she cupped him intimately. She hated the fact that he was beating himself up over this. "You made me a woman," she filled in helpfully, "And it's okay, really."

He shook his head against her. "Damn it all. You kept saying you were ready, coming on to me. I assumed..."

Her eyes widened, listening to his mutterings issued so close to her face. He smelled like butterscotch, and she had a really stunning close-up view of his rugged face. Her wet sex clamped down on him again, adjusting to the size of him, and she let out a gasp of pleasure, but still he didn't move. Damn it all, he was rejecting her again. Apparently, liar her, wasn't experienced enough for the stud PI. Well that was too damned bad. He'd better put out this ache. She sighed in humiliation and admitted defeat. "Well get off me then if I'm not woman enough for you, Lucas."

His eyes opened, and he speared her with a pissed off, turned on, resigned, "you're really gonna get it" look that made her shiver with delight and her sex ripple around him.

He shook his head. "Not female enough? Love, do you really have no idea of your allure or is this just another lie?"

She blinked back tears. There was no way she would answer that humiliating question. Allure? Her? Was he crazy? But the hungry look in his eyes told her he meant it.

"Well hell, I'm a dead man anyway," he gritted out, bending to kiss her.

Dead man! She moaned into his mouth as he ground the base of his cock against her clit, and she burned, gasping with pleasure. Charity melted as his lips claimed hers and her sex loosened, letting him sink into her another inch.

"That's it, doll, open for me, let me inside. Your sweet pussy was made for me," he groaned rocking into her.

She whimpered, loosening at his encouraging words. He growled, surging the rest of the way inside until his balls slapped against her wet labia. She gasped, quivering around him. Yes, she was made for him!

"God, it's so good." He went still, resting inside her.

She whimpered, shock waves going off inside her pussy as her sex stretched wide open. He lay still, letting her get used to his size, as he kissed her thoroughly. Now this was more like it.

His tongue rubbed teasingly along hers, his hand cupped the side of her breast, his fingertip brushing teasingly against her nipple, and then slipped down to tease her clit. She moaned, her body blazing.

"Wrap your sweet legs around me, doll, take me home."

She sobbed, doing as he said, wrapping her legs around his middle, moaning when it shifted him inside her sex. And then he pulled out to surge back into her. Charity cried out, meeting his thrusts, her smacking wetly against him as her hips snapped up to meet him. She saw stars, his shaft pressing against her burning clit with every stroke. She closed her eyes, her legs squeezing around his tight buns as he rammed into her, and she screamed his name as she came. Strong waves of her orgasm clenched him hard, and she heard him groan as she lost consciousness. Her last memory was of hearing Lucas growl while feeling his cock jerk hard inside her as he came and came and came.

Chapter 5

Lucas lay there stunned, clutching a semi-conscious Charity to his side. It was their way when females came into their powers, but it scared the hell out of him. Then she snored, and he smiled, relaxing as he stroked her silky skin, hardly able to believe he was in her bed. He tenderly smoothed a hand down her curves, trying to come to terms with what just happened. What she'd just pushed him to do. But he didn't regret it, no matter what. Still, he knew he was toast. Hell, he'd just had the impudence to take a princess early and he was willing to pay the penalty.

His mouth twisted with self-mocking. Charles Langford would probably slit his throat for jumping the gun and taking her early, and he had it coming. Still, he wouldn't change a thing, as she murmured, nestling her sweet body close to his. Her ass rocked back against his rousing manhood as if begging for more, and his randy cock thrummed against her sultry heat. He groaned, pressing against her heat, leaning forward to taste her nape, licking her. She sighed with pleasure and he smiled. The heady sense of satisfaction running through him was intoxicating, almost as intoxicating as his mate.

The scent of their joining still hung in the air, leaving him a little drunk on her pheromones. But he didn't have time to give into his body's primal demands to taste her passion again. Regretfully, he pulled away from Charity and slipped from bed, tucking the covers around her. She'd sleep for hours after her first joining, giving him time to work. He was going to need help to deal with Kill, but not from the Langford Clan. He still wasn't sure if he could trust anyone there. Besides, they hadn't even smelled the Betas in their midst this morning, so how much help would they be?

He strode nude from Charity's suite into his adjoining rooms, his mind back on his mission, his black jeans materializing on him in the process. He pulled his laptop out from behind the sofa where he'd hidden it and logged on, messaging the only people he could trust. *Bran, I need a hand, bring Garth,* he typed, trying to decide how he could explain it all to his far flung Alpha compatriots. A burning sensation in the skin over his heart made him rub the sting away and look down at his chest. He smiled, wishing it was Charity's love bite, although he'd had to restrain himself because her touch drove him wild, and he didn't want to hurt her. Instead, all he'd allowed her was her hot legs wrapped around him as he thrust into her and the milking heat of her vagina.

He looked down at the spot in stunned disbelief as red entwined hearts appeared directly above his left nipple, like an embossed tattoo that was anything but human. A Wolfen mating mark! It couldn't be, and it sure as hell shouldn't be there, but there it was, burning into his flesh just the same. It had to be a fluke, a trick of the fates who'd always seemed to have it in for him. Because there was no way Charity would carry the same mark, and even if by some strange miracle she did, it wasn't binding for her. Elite and Alpha females always had the option of refusing their beloveds. He was well and truly screwed, and he knew it.

What's up, Lobo?

Lucas put his mind off his grim, sexless future to read Bran's smart ass reply. Lobo indeed, Bran knew damned well he hated that title. *I need back up in Vegas ASAP.*

Why, do you need help at the tables? Gambling is for fools. The odds are against you, pal.

Boy, didn't he know it. The odds of coming out of this with his manhood and heart intact were nil, but he could damn well come out of this with his mate intact. *I need your help guarding a princess. Kill and a hunting pack are on the scene.* He waited and after what he assumed was stunned silence on the other end, Bran typed in:

So, the rumors are true. You are mated to a Langford Princess.

Are you coming or not? Lucas asked, rather than answer the question, not surprised that rumors of his mission had spread. No wonder Kill had been wary enough to avoid him earlier when he'd tried to hunt the bastard down. But that was before Charity had arrived on the scene, slipping the detail of Elites he'd had surrounding her. That and what had just happened in the bedroom had changed the dynamics.

Of course I'm coming. I wouldn't miss getting a glimpse of one of the Langford Princesses for anything. I'll be there with back up in a flash, literally.

Lucas winced at the teasing. *I wouldn't miss getting a glimpse of one of the Langford Princesses for anything. Charity is way more than that. She is warm, feisty, smart, life itself.*

Hell, Lucas felt jealous of his friend wanting to see her, he realized ruefully, of another man wanting a glimpse of her. He had it bad. Crap! *Get your fucking head on straight, wolf,* he scolded himself. He looked up, satisfied, when with a crackle of static electricity, Bran and Garth materialized in the room. At least he had backup. Bran, was dressed in a staid three-piece suit. Garth popped in bare-ass naked as usual because he couldn't time jump worth a damn and he was bitching a blue streak. Lucas smirked. It was good to know that some things never changed.

Garth growled and grabbed a pillow off the bed, stuffing it in front of his crotch. "Damn it, Bran, next time you dematerialize me without notice, I'm going for your throat, you dumb ass banker."

"Hey, there was no time to waste, surf bum."

"Remind me to burn that," Lucas commented, slanting a pointed look at the pillow Garth was hiding his junk behind. Garth scowled at him and zapped a loud Hawaiian shirt and cut offs on his stocky body. Then he flicked the lace trimmed pillow back onto the bed with a smirk.

"Damn, man I was having a perfect day. What's this all about, Lucas?" Garth demanded.

"He needs us to guard his woman," Bran cut in, wincing at Garth's loud get up. "Geeze, Scooby Doo, you could at least try to look good."

Garth flipped Bran the bird then boldly looked through the open doorway to see Charity sleeping. "So the rumors are true."

Lucas growled even though he knew the wolf wouldn't poach.

"Down boy," Bran said with a grin as he stared at Charity too. "We just never saw a princess in the flesh before."

"And you're not going to this time." Lucas said, stalking past them to quietly shut the door so the loudmouths wouldn't wake her. He was going to have enough explaining to do as it was, when she found out. He didn't need adding the comedy pairings of his compatriots to the mix. "We'll need to set up a perimeter guard. Kill's in the hotel." He didn't miss the fury in their eyes at the mention of their nemesis. They all had good reason to hate Kill. Lucas grimaced when they both stared grimly at his mating mark.

Garth whistled and Bran muttered. "Well I'll be damned."

Garth grinned. "You already are, buddy." He turned to Lucas. "What about her? Does she have one?"

Lucas's frowned, wishing he knew, but afraid to find out. "Don't know yet, but I doubt it."

"Does she know what it means?" Bran asked.

"No, and you'd damned well better not tell her."

"And let her turn you into a gelding? No way. I'm not keeping silent, Lobo," Bran said scowling.

Lucas gave him a repressive frown that had him sighing in defeat. "It's not your problem. Don't make it one between me and you."

*****

Charity rolled over in bed. Her hand came down on Lucas's cold, empty pillow beside her, and she let out a cry of regret. He was gone! She came instantly awake in a pained rush, looking around for confirmation, even though she knew it in her heart. Why? It seemed like history repeating itself, reminding her of his defection yesterday.

Why hadn't Lucas stuck around for the morning after? She frowned at the bright daylight shining through the windows. Good grief how long had she slept? And more importantly, when did he leave? She sat up in bed with a gasp, feeling a small twinge from her nether regions. Even though he'd vanished, he'd left a lasting impression. She'd been thoroughly debauched by Lucas Kendal last night, and she'd loved it.

Well, at least she wasn't a thirty-two-year-old virgin anymore. That was something to celebrate. The sheets rubbed erotically against her sensitized nipples, making them tingle and her breath catch as she pulled them up to her chin. It was his fault that one taste of Lucas's fierce lovemaking had only made her hungrier for more. She closed her eyes with a sigh, remembering his mouth on her, sucking her nipples hard, making her squirm on the sheets as he'd restrained her, forcing her to feel it all.

The low, masculine sound of a throat being cleared let her know she wasn't alone. She spun to look at the doorway, feeling vulnerable. Her heart tripped with gladness as she focused on Lucas standing by the door with two steaming cups of coffee in his big hands. He was dressed all in black again and he looked good enough to eat. Too bad he hadn't let her taste him last night, but she had every hope of rectifying that situation now.

He arched a raven brow as if reading her mind again. How did he do it? And how had he appeared so instantly, so stealthily? She hadn't heard the door open. Gazing into the whiskey-dark depths of his eyes as he pinned her with a possessive look, she acknowledged that there was definitely something deliciously spooky, otherworldly about him. "Where did you come from?" she asked, knowing he'd fob her off with a lie.

"I just popped in with coffee for you, doll."

She took a deep whiff of the heady aroma as he approached the bed with his peace offering.

"Cinnamon Mocha, yum. This is my favorite blend. How did you know?"

"I'm observant, I guess. It is part of my job description after all, doll," he answered with a shrug.

"My hero," she teased, feeling brighter now that he was with her. She watched him flush at the compliment. He really was her hero after saving her from the rogue hackers last night, not to mention rocking her world when he made her a woman. It seemed the man wasn't used to praise.

"I'm no hero." He thrust the cup at her. Two droplets plopped onto the sheets soaking her skin and she winced at the burn.

"Ouch," she said, brushing them away.

"Oh shit, I'm sorry, Charity. Are you okay?" His brow wrinkled as he set the coffee down and tugged back the sheet to look at her.

She blushed when Lucas bared her breasts with a tug, still feeling shy even after last night. "I'm fine Lucas. It just made me jump," she said, ignoring the burn in her skin so he wouldn't feel even worse about dripping coffee on her. She needn't have bothered fibbing, seeing the scowl on his face when he looked at her chest. Oh shit was she badly burned? If anything her skin was hotter, scorching. She sighed, watching his expression turn from concern, to shock, to resolve, and looked down to see what worried him. Her eyes widened with surprise to see it wasn't a coffee spill that was stinging; it was some kind of weirdly hickey. When the heck had he given her that? It got darker as she watched, forming into an embossed heart shape. She smirked, wondering how he'd managed that in the dark. "You seem to have put your mark on me, Lucas."

"So I notice," he said, adding soberly, "This is all my fault. I'm sorry."

Why was he so worried about her reaction to a little rough love bite? She wasn't a fragile little princess and she wouldn't have him thinking otherwise. "It certainly is, you beast," she teased trying to lighten the mood. "I must have been the last thirty-two-year-old virgin in Vegas, but that's all changed thanks to you."

"Are you sure you're okay?"

"Never better," she said pulling back the sheets for him, loving the way he sucked in a breath and watched her. She didn't miss the fire in his eyes when he looked at her, either. They scorched a path from her hickey to her stiff nipples to her sex, now quivering and getting wet for him. "Are you coming back to bed?"

He hesitated for a moment and then smiled. "Love, I don't think any power on Earth could stop me from doing that."

She giggled when he bent down and picked her up, scooping her out of bed. Then it dawned on her that he was going to carry her nude through the suite while he remained dressed. "We're going to do it in the bathroom," she said with a shocked gasp as he stepped into the room.

"Damn straight. I aim to have you in every room in this suite." He strode to the shower. "Turn it on."

There were two ways to take that and she chose the naughty one. She smiled impishly and reached down to touch his rousing cock through his jeans, making him growl. "I think I already did." She grinned as his heavy shaft lengthened under her palm.

"Just so you realize, every time you touch me you bring out the beast in me," he warned.

Heck that's what she was counting on. Why the warning? "Good!"

At his brooding look she stopped fondling him long enough to turn on the shower. He stepped them into the double marble stall, still holding her tight in his arms, still fully fucking dressed. Oh god! It was the most romantic thing that had ever happened to her. She pressed tight to his hot, wet body, the rough tee shirt and jeans abrading her skin. Lucas kissed her and then released her to slowly let her slide down his aroused body, and she gasped. Her sensitized nipples raked teasingly against his black denim shirt, tugging, lengthening, driving her wild, and then her mound encountered his hard, wet denim-covered cock and she groaned. Rubbing herself shamelessly on him her sex clenched.

Lucas growled, kissing her deep as he clutched her bottom and pulled her tight to the hard ridge of his cock. She moaned into his mouth and rocked her sensitized clit against him until she was melting. He did it harder, and she came, throwing back her head to howl. He let out a grunt and spun her weak, shuddering body, around to lower her onto all fours on the wet shower's tile floor, sinking to his knees behind her. "What are you doing?"

"I'm going to take you my way, Charity, doll. It's called wolf or doggy style. You'll have to tell me how you like it."

She shuddered in eager anticipation when she heard his zipper jerk down and then the thick head of his cock butted up against her pussy from behind, and her mind went a little haywire. Oh lord, it was so primitive and so good. Then he clasped her hips and thrust into her hard, and she moaned, taking him deep. Arching her back, she bopped back on his cock, meeting his swift strokes, on fire for him. It gave him greater access and he penetrated her deeper, seeming to reach to her cervix, driving her wild. Oh gads, it almost felt like he was growing bigger as her sex clutched him hard. She lost track of thoughts as he cupped her breasts pinching the nipples firmly. She moaned as it tugged on her sex and she rippled around him. Then he slicked a hand between her legs to stroke her clit in time with his thrusts.

Trembling on the brink, she was dimly aware of her skin heating up under the waterfall, her limbs changing. Dizzy and in love, she still felt a strong sense of power sweeping through her, felt his cock grow even more inside her to the point of painfulness. Wet, furry limbs rubbed together as he slammed into her harder, nipping gently at her nape when she inched away and her cunt grew around him to accommodate him.

He pressed her clit firmly, and she came with a growl, her stronger sexual spasms pulling him deep inside her again and again as she came for what seemed like forever. Time hung suspended as she pulsed, flickering back and forth between animal and human, coming longer and harder than ever before. He let out a howl coming high and hard behind her, holding her tight as he emptied inside her. She passed out, totally spent.

She didn't know how much later, but she came awake cradled in Lucas's arms. Warmly swaddled in a thick terry cloth robe, she noticed that he was wearing one too, and he was sitting in a chair holding her in his lap. He was watching her, staring at her in a panic actually, which stunned her. She must have given him quite a scare. She gave him a wobbly smile hoping to reassure him. "That was some great idea of yours, Lucas Kendal. You seem to have sent me reeling."

He closed his eyes and crushed her to him, hugging her tight. "You scared the hell out of me, doll."

She gasped for breath in his tight hold. The man didn't know his own strength. Then she recalled her own burst of strength before she swooned. What was going on with her? She pushed him back a little. "I'm okay, but I think there's something weird going on with me." His troubled frown seemed to give credence to her thoughts, but then he smiled tenderly.

"On the contrary, I think there's something wonderful going on with you, doll."

"You do huh," she murmured reaching out to touch his face and dip her finger into the sexy dimple in his chin.

"Yes. It'll be an adjustment period for you of course, but you'll come out of it on top and the stronger for it."

"Speaking of on top," she cooed rubbing against him, then caught sight of the clock. "Oh good grief it's after ten. Why didn't you wake me earlier?"

He arched a brow. "I made a command decision, doll. I decided you needed your sleep more than your morning sessions."

"Well, I've got a seminar to teach this afternoon," she said wondering if she could cure him of his arrogant tendencies. But they were part of what she loved about him.

"Cancel it."

"I can't. Everyone's curious about my fireball program." She stared down his forbidding look. Just because he'd taught her the joys of sex didn't mean he could boss her around.

"I'll just bet they are. Ever think your inclusion in the program might have brought your hackers out of the woodwork?"

She sucked in a shocked breath at the statement and flashed a plaintive look his way. "Oh no, do you really think so." At his dark look she sighed. There was no way she could put him and her staff in danger. Even if it meant cancelling her presentation, so be it. "I'll cancel my presentation."

He shook his head. "Not necessary. I'll be with you every step of the way."

She bit her lip. "I can't put you in that kind of danger."

He smiled and enfolded her in his arms. "Don't worry about me. I can take care of myself."

Chapter 6

Charity walked back to her conference table after presenting her session outlining her fireball program. The sun was beginning to go down and they only had an hour to go before the end of the conference. They'd made it, seeing that there'd been no sign of the rogue hackers all day. She sighed with relief while her staff members beamed at her, seeming to relax. Good! Her presentation had been a hit and they could all let down their guards. With Lucas sitting there looking menacing if anyone so much as frowned at her, the hackers would have to be stupid to try anything.

When she approached her table she noticed a darkly tanned stocky man wearing a loud Hawaiian shirt leaned against the back wall staring at her. She suspected that he and a preppy type in a suit had taken turns tailing her all afternoon. It wasn't the scary sexual stare of the trio last night, but it was just as intense, maybe even a bit angry, like he disapproved of her for some reason. It was probably just paranoia on her part, she decided when he looked away.

He didn't really fit in with the computer nerds like her. Maybe he was a spouse of an attendee. No, he had the same focused look in his eye that Lucas wore when he was working. Her gaze shifted to Lucas, sprawled at a corner conference table watching her like he dared anyone to make a false move. Maybe the guy was another hired gun? That settled in her mind, she smiled at Lucas who stood when she approached, pulled out her chair, and seated her. He'd been so attentive today, just like a real boyfriend and not a paid employee. "Thanks."

"You're welcome, doll, you were great."

Looking deep into his eyes, Charity lost herself in his gaze, feeling warmed by his approval. Soon, this weekend affair would be over. It pained her to think it. "Only one more night and we go back to reality."

"Good."

Startled by the vehemence of his words she couldn't stop the disappointment from being reflected in her voice. "I'm sorry. I didn't think you were that eager to go home."

He shrugged, scanning the crowd. "It's easier to guard you there."

It was all business then. Charity couldn't help feeling crestfallen. As if he read her mind, he focused on her, frowning.

"We've still got tonight, doll."

It might be all she could get from him. Her heart tripping at the thought, she edged closer to him, her thigh pressing against his. She might not have him forever, but they had tonight, and she'd make the most of those magical hours. The Hawaiian shirt inched closer, focused, his full attention on them. "Don't look now but I think we're being spied on." Lucas tensed beside her and looked in the other direction toward the French doors facing the back gardens. "No, eight o'clock to your left. The guy in the loud shirt."

He seemed to relax at her words and looked over her shoulder.

"Don't worry, I can take him."

No way was she letting him get in a fistfight on her account. "Not funny," she said watching his eyes narrow.

"I've got something I need to take care of. You stay here and I'll be back to fetch you at the end of the session. I've made reservations at eight for dinner tonight."

Something was wrong, she could sense it. "I mean it. You're not going to go pick a fight with that guy," she said with a forbidding frown.

"I wouldn't dream of it. Humor me, okay."

"Okay," she agreed, bemused and in love.

Half an hour later, the conference room cleared and there was still no sign of Lucas. He must have gotten tied up with his secret business. With little other choice, she walked out of the room alone and made her way to the restaurant. They had reservations at eight. He'd have to show up for that.

She couldn't help being worried about him as she strode down the corridor toward the restaurant, knowing only something dire would have kept him from her. Walking by the glass doors facing the back garden, she heard a howl that stopped her in her tracks. A wolf in Las Vegas? Impossible, but she felt compelled to look just the same as she heard another howl. She'd always been drawn to animals, especially wolves, volunteering at a rescue unit that worked to save wolves in the wild. She pushed open the glass door and stepped out into the cool Nevada evening, shivering a little. She rubbed her hands up and down her bare arms, listening.

Growls and snarls were louder out here. A few steps down the path took her into a clearing, and she froze. Wolves were indeed in Las Vegas, and they were vicious from the look of them. There were five of them in total and they were fighting. A large black and a scraggly speckled one doggedly went after a smaller gray wolf while off to the left a slightly larger gray wolf tangled with another scraggly speckled one.

Two viciously attacked one smaller one, and she cried out in sympathy, her mind scrambling for a way to stop the fight. Then a large timber wolf bounded out of the bushes, pulling the biggest beast off the one being attacked. Her heart in her throat, she watched them go at each other, knowing there was nothing she could do to stop it, just wait around to pick up the pieces. The timber's side was slashed at viciously. Just then, a side door opened, spilling out the casino sounds. The noise and light seemed to shock the wolves into immobility for a moment.

She used the opportunity to pick up a heavy glass ashtray from a patio table and hurl it at the vicious black one. It bonked him on the head. He let out a snarl, turned to bare his teeth at her and then skulked away into the night, the two dark ones at his side.

The timber turned his head to stare at her, his sides heaving. The two gray wolves he'd defended hung back in the shadows. A charge, that had little to do with fear, went through her as his soulful eyes locked with hers. She didn't pick up any vicious vibes off the timber, just annoyance. Why should he be annoyed? She'd saved his hide, kind of. At least she'd caused a diversion and broken up the fight.

A glance at the bleeding wound at his side made her wince in sympathy. He could bleed to death or get an infection. Could she possibly get him to a vet? The rescue team she worked with might have some contacts in the area.

"Here boy," she said softly to gauge his reaction. He took a cautious step toward her his tail wagging slowly. It was a good sign. Maybe he'd been someone's pet, or gotten loose from a petting zoo. She felt his pack's wary gazes on her but didn't sense danger, mostly stunned curiosity as they stood back watching.

As he stepped closer, she got a good look at him. He was a handsome specimen, and his intelligent dark eyes drew her in. Not picking up any bad vibes, she wasn't afraid. "Are you okay, boy?" She held out her hand, palm up, for him to sniff, which he obediently did, even giving her fingers a little lick with his rough tongue. *Just so he doesn't think I'm finger licking good.* As if he could read her mind he rubbed his muzzle against her most affectionately. She patted him on the back, assessing his injuries, and he shoved his muzzle against her palm and sniffed her. "I love you too," she said with a giggle as he licked her again. "Now, I've got to figure out a way to get you to the vet."

At the word "vet," he stopped licking her hand and loped away before she could stop him. It confirmed her suspicion that he was a pet. He knew the word vet. The timber wolf stopped at the trees, looked back at her, and then he was gone. She sighed, wishing she could have done more for him. Maybe it was for the best. A wild beast could usually take care of himself. Shrugging, she turned to go back into the building, realizing it was past time for her to meet Lucas for dinner.

Charity let herself back into the warmth and noise of the hotel. She wouldn't miss all the noisy clanging slot machines when they went home tomorrow, she decided with a wry twist of her lips. She hurried to the restaurant, but Lucas wasn't there yet.

She sat at their table waiting for him, her mind still on the timber wolf that got away. She hoped it would be okay. Then the guy in the Hawaiian shirt and the man in the suit ambled into the restaurant and made their way to the bar. She couldn't help being conscious of their quizzical gazes as they passed. Hawaiian shirt looked even more disheveled than before, and the guy in the suit had a black eye, and he was breathing hard like he'd been jogging. Oh no, they and Lucas hadn't gotten into a fistfight, had they? That might explain why Lucas had vanished. She'd put her foot down against that kind of thing, even if Lucas were doing it for the right reasons.

As if thinking of him drew him to her, Lucas walked into the room. His gaze locked with hers and she read more than heat in them; she read gratitude and what looked like admiration. Maybe they did have a chance after all. When he walked toward her, she noticed him moving a bit stiffly. "Are you okay, honey?"

"Honey," he said slowly as if he was savoring the love name. "I like that."

"Good, now answer my question," she said as he sat. When he slashed a look at Hawaiian-shirt dude, she realized she'd been right, he'd been fighting. "I told you not to fight with him."

He stiffened when the Hawaiian shirt wearer chuckled then frowned at him repressively. "Honey, you don't get to tell me how to do my job."

She glared back at the two arrogant males as they shared a private joke. "When you work for me, yes, I do have the right to tell you how to do your job." She slanted a scowl at the man at the bar who straight out howled with laughter at her statement. The shuttered look Lucas gave her made her want to take back the words, but she'd been scared for him. Certainly he could see that couldn't he? She reached out to touch his rigid hand. "I'm sorry...I didn't mean..."

"Don't worry about it, Princess," he said grimly.

Oh no, she couldn't believe he was shutting her out like this. And what was all this princess business about? They were back to her being the boss's daughter and him being the hired gun. At least it seemed so in his mind, even though she hadn't meant it that way. She squeezed his hand, refusing to let go, and then a rank, horribly familiar smell wafted into the room. She wrinkled her nose and turned to see the rogue hackers strut into the room with Kill at their lead. Lucas growled, pulling his hand from hers and turned to scowl at them.

Charity realized Lucas was ready to pull out a gun if she was threatened and her heart stopped. She put two and two together and realized they were who Lucas was fighting with, not his seeming antagonist at the bar. She passed a dismissive glance over the pesky hackers, sure they wouldn't try anything in public and feeling confident with Lucas by her side. Still, it tore at her that he could have gotten badly hurt because of her. "You got in a fight with them, didn't you?"

He shrugged. "I won."

"That's a matter of opinion, Lobo," Kill said in an accented growl as he walked over to them.

"Lobo?" she asked.

"A nickname," Lucas bit out.

"Then you do know him."

"Allow me to introduce myself. Kill Angus, at your service, lass."

"You're not welcome here, Kill."

Kill shook his head. "See what I mean? Such bad manners. I was just about to ask Miss Langford out for dinner and dancing."

"No thank you." Charity drew back. Something predatory flared in Kill's spooky light blue eyes at the rejection. "And I'll thank you not to beat up my boyfriend."

Kill chuckled. "Your boyfriend, how precious is that. Let me tell you all about..."

Lucas growled low in his throat, moving toward him. The man with the Hawaiian shirt and the man in the dark suit stepped forward menacingly to back up Lucas, and Kill's mouth snapped shut.

Kill bowed. "Madame, I'll bow to your tender sensibilities, for now."

Charity took in the two men standing menacingly behind Lucas, as Kill slunk out of the room, his companions at his heels. "His nickname is Kill," she said dryly.

"Yup, hung on him by his crazy bastard of a father, Rowan."

"Charming." She rolled her eyes. "I assume these two gentlemen are your back up helpers. Introduce me, won't you."

The two men fidgeted while the blond actually blushed.

"These two are Bran and Garth. Two friends I can count on in a dark corner."

"It's a pleasure to meet you," she said, adding, "Thanks for taking care of my boyfriend."

Garth shook his head. "Us take care of him? It's the other way around, Princess."

Bran elbowed him in the ribs. "Stop babbling and say thank you, stupid."

Garth glared at him then turned back to smile at her. "Thank you."

"Would you like to join us for dinner," she offered, seeing Lucas frown. "Honey, don't scowl at your friends."

"No thanks," Bran said with a grin. "We're on duty."

Garth loped after him, complaining loudly, "But I'm hungry."

*****

Lucas's sensitive hearing picked up their short argument and continued amusement at his expense as they walked toward the bar. He didn't really mind, owing them more than he could repay in one lifetime. Bran was a healer and had already worked on his wound, cauterizing it. By morning, it would be mostly healed.

He sat back and looked at Charity as she went back to scanning the menu. She was very serene for a woman who'd witnessed a pack attack, come to his wolf rescue, and then been hit on by Kill. She'd called him boy and petted him; he still couldn't wrap his mind around it. On the plus side, she liked wolves, so maybe finding out she was one wouldn't be such a blow after all. God he hoped so because she was the prettiest wolf he'd ever seen. When she'd flickered and turned in the shower, she'd taken his breath away, though he knew she didn't remember it.

"So tell me about them," she said, putting down her menu and glancing at Bran and Garth as they bellied up to the bar.

Lucas gave them a wry glance noting that their fierce glares sent the other patrons scurrying to the other end of the bar. "Not very subtle, are they?"

"No, but effective I'd say. We should give them a bonus for clearing the room."

He frowned at her teasing words, suddenly reminded that he was only hired help. "They aren't doing this for money. We're friends and have each other's backs in time of trouble."

"So they're PI's too?"

He chuckled at the thought of them taking up his lowly profession. "Hardly. Garth is a surf bum, in case you hadn't guessed."

"Don't tell me, Hawaii."

"How'd you guess," he said smiling at Garth's casual attire. He'd chosen to fight his private demons by not caring about anything while Bran had decided to kill Wall Street, literally. "Bran's an investment banker."

"Figures, the tailored three-piece suits a dead giveaway, Saville Row unless I miss my guess." She turned to look at Lucas. "Tell me about this Kill guy."

Sure, she'd know about expensive suits and all the trappings of wealth, just like the Elite mate her father would eventually choose for her. The thought pissed him off to no end, but he forced himself to relax, sit back, and address her question. It just might save her life. "Stay away from him, Princess, he's bad news." He saw her scowl at the princess jibe and smiled, glad to see her worry replaced by anger. Anger he could deal with.

"I already figured that out for myself, stud," she snapped, slanting him an assessing look as she said, "He seemed to know you pretty well."

So she wanted answers. Well, she was entitled. "He should, we're bastard half-brothers along with about a quarter of the members of our clan. Our dad was real good at procreating you see," he admitted, seeing her eyes widen with shock. Then he tossed in the kicker. "And dear old Dad would like nothing better than to see me dead. Hell, it's Kill's fondest wish too."

*****

Charity tried to wrap her mind around his bomb of a statement. It was shocking, inconceivable, considering the sheltering, loving family she was part of. She leaned forward in sympathy, covering his hand with hers, and he pulled away as if he couldn't stand her touch. "I'm so sorry."

"Don't be. It made me the...*man*...I am today. Besides, I got out okay and I'm still breathing."

She squeezed his hand, feeling him stiffen up at the comforting gesture. "Do you want to talk about it?"

"No, and I don't want you to fret about it either. Let's enjoy the last night here. You're mine, at least for tonight anyway, and I mean to make the most of it."

Chapter 7

Back in the suite, Lucas took his time undressing Charity. He wanted to memorize the experience and every sweet inch of her body. She smiled up at him like she was drinking in the sun. He felt a pang deep inside. "Thank you," he murmured as she leaned into his touch with a moan.

"For what?" She nuzzled his chin, her tongue dipping into the cleft, making his cock jerk.

He smiled, cupping the lush globes of her ass and pulling her to him. "For wanting me as much as I want you, doll, it's a new experience for me."

"How could I not want you like crazy?" She nibbled on his lip while starting to unbutton his shirt. "You're drop dead sexy and you're mine, aren't you?"

"For as long as you'll have me." Lucas groaned then froze when she frantically reached up to unbutton his shirt. Shit, if she took off his shirt, she'd see his mating mark, the wound, and it would be all over for him. "Hands off," he said sternly giving her a dominant look to convey his mood. She got it in a heartbeat when her hands dropped to her sides and her pulse ratcheted up. He couldn't resist smiling when she gave him a feisty scowl despite her arousal.

She tapped her toe impatiently as her eyes ate him up. "What are you trying to do, Lucas Kendal, talk me out of seducing you again?"

He smirked. "Not hardly, doll, but I set the pace," he said, pulling her to him to kiss her while his open hand smacked her ass, and she yelped into his mouth. Then she moaned as he rubbed away the sting. No way was he going to allow anything to get in the way of this moment. He deepened the kiss and she sucked on his tongue almost making him come in his pants. He broke the kiss and looked into her sultry eyes, carrying a feminine mystery as old as time. "I want your sweet mouth on me," he said letting her decide if she'd surrender.

"Finally," she said sinking to her knees in front of him. "If you dare say I'm not ready for this step, I'll kick your manly ass. Got that?"

He chuckled at her vehemence, knowing she wanted this as much as he did. "Got it."

"Damned straight," she said mimicking him as she lowered his zipper and freed his cock. She pushed his pants down under his balls and leaned back on her heels, feasting her eyes on him.

He groaned, the head of his cock jerking up for her as she made him wait. "Well, are you going down on that or not?" he challenged and saw her eyes darken with heat.

She slanted him a hot look then flicked her tongue out to taste his slit, letting out a yummy noise. He groaned at the heated vibration and then she swirled her wet tongue around the head of his cock like she was polishing the tip, savoring his flavor and he swore. "Show me how hard you can suck, doll."

She flicked up an annoyed look at being rushed then moaned when she opened wide and took him inside, sucking so hard on the head he crossed his eyes. He howled with pleasure and longing. "Oh, doll, that is so good." He groaned as her tongue flicked the underside of his cock and swirled around the head, and then she took him back into her mouth deeper yet.

Moaning, he felt his cock grow larger, his Wolfen arousal kicking in, and gently disengaged from her so as not to hurt her. Wolf cocks grew, locking them inside the female they were mating with until they emptied their seed; it was the nature of the beast he was.

"You're getting bigger," she said with surprise, staring at his throbbing cock as it grew in front of her. "I thought I felt that before in the shower."

He drew her up off the floor and carried her to the bed, flicking off the bedside lamp and feeling the beast rage within him. She shouldn't have had the presence of mind to remember that. It just went to show how powerful a Wolfen female she was becoming.

Sprawling on the bed with her, he plunged into her warmth, and her pussy tightened around him as she wet the head of his dick with her juices. Sensing the imminent change in her, he reversed positions. She knelt on the edge, and he drove into her from behind as she changed into a beautiful female timber wolf before his eyes.

Howling, he pounded into her harder, deeper, feeling her sex grow to hold him tight as a vise grip. She threw back her head and came with a howl that was music to his primal ears, setting off his own explosion of cum. With his jerking cock lodged deep inside her squeezing pussy he growled with pleasure, slowly pouring out his tribute to her. Closing his eyes, he force-blocked the memory from her. Then he rocked inside her as she milked every last drop from him, savoring this moment of mutual extended Wolfen orgasm.

*****

Charity showered and dressed the next day after a lazy morning of breakfast in bed with Lucas, feeling better and more energized than she had in years. It must have been the mind numbing sex. Try as she might to recall the details of their joining last night, she couldn't.

The shower shut off in Lucas's room and she smiled, picturing him naked and glistening. Now those water drops she'd like to lick off him and then drop to her knees and suck him off again, and maybe make his eyes cross again. She chuckled. At least that part she remembered. And the way he woke her this morning, fully dressed and lying between her legs and tasting her to his heart's content until she was squirming and out of her head.

She'd finally allowed him to escape to shower, dress, and pack. They'd be cutting it close to make their flight. As usual, Lucas had their departure planned like a military maneuver. The man was definitely paranoid, but she could make allowances for his overprotective streak. Smoothing the wrinkles out of her challis print sundress, she stepped in front of the mirror to fasten her ruby necklace, wanting to look especially nice for Lucas. She looked at her smiling reflection, trying to reconcile the sexually experienced woman with the old maid she'd been before. Maybe they'd make good on her fantasy about the mile high club.

Pulling her suitcase from the closet, she laid it on the rumpled bed, recalling their morning delight. Time to get packed. She flipped open the case and went to the dresser. Light glinted off her closed laptop computer. Her laird. Since she'd been with Lucas, she hadn't given him a thought. She had to break it off with her laird. It was the right thing to do; besides, it wasn't in her to juggle two lovers, even if one was only the cyber sort.

She opened the laptop and went directly to the site, logging in as *Sugar,* and then groaned when she saw that he wasn't there. She didn't have much time; Lucas was out of the shower and would be here soon. A moment later, *Wolf* logged in and she smiled. *Please follow me to our private room, my laird.*

What is it, Sugar? We don't have a date today.

There aren't going to be any more dates. She sighed. *There's no easy way to say this...*

You've found someone else.

How did he know? *As usual, you're very perceptive.*

But not perceptive enough to keep you, I see.

She heard the wry humor in her laird's voice. *I'm sorry.*

Tell me about my rival.

He's, um ...he's...

Nice.

I wouldn't call him nice. He's my mate.

That's a bit of an old-fashioned term.

I guess it is, but it fits the way that I feel. A thud from Lucas's room caught her attention. Was he already packed? She walked to his door.

Well I guess it's time for me to—

She tried the knob. It wasn't locked. Lucas, back turned to her, was at the desk using a laptop computer. She stared at him, her jaw dropping to see the man who was supposed to be computer illiterate using one. Her sense of betrayal was complete when he spoke.

"—bow out to the better man."

"Why?" she let out a strangled whisper.

He stiffened. What did he hope to accomplish by this deception? To get into her pants? All he'd had to do was ask and she'd have been his. Surely he knew that. Damn, she felt like a fool. Lucas spun in her direction. The irritation and resolve on his face made her even angrier as her heart broke.

"Now, doll, I can explain..."

"Save it, I'm not interested." She started to shut the door.. "Give me some privacy while I finish packing."

"I'll be right outside your door."

The promise tugged at her heartstrings, but she turned and locked the connecting door anyway. How could she have been so blind? Sex, hormones, love, her heart sank at the last one. Blinking tears away, she started throwing clothes in her suitcase. Damn the man for toying with her affections this way. She'd been so easily managed, so eager to believe his lies. This tore it. When she got home, she'd see him fired if it was the last thing she did. He'd even lied about his lack of computer skills; he was talking to her without a headphone and mike. Even she wasn't that good.

The overpowering scent of spilled perfume covering something foul suddenly filled the air, and her nose wrinkled as her stomach clenched. A muffled thud behind her told her she wasn't alone. Lucas, damn it. How dare he invade her space this way when she'd expressly forbade it. He hadn't even honored her request for privacy. Furious, she spun around to see Kill standing inside her room, inches from her, with a gloating smile. She opened up her mouth to scream as something pricked her shoulder and unseen hands grabbed her from behind. Everything went black, cutting off her scream.

Charity came to moments later, her stomach cramping, and feeling totally disoriented. Birds singing, and a brisk breeze billowing her dress around her legs all told her she was outside. But where? Her nose wrinkled against the vile smell of the two hulking men dragging her along a path. She winced when her toes caught on a rut and her shoulders almost pulled out of their sockets.

Dragged past a workroom, she spied a modern computer inside. The smoking mainframe was torn apart. A technician with long unkempt hair, dressed in a ragged kilt, gave her a scowl as she passed. Did the fireball she'd launched against the hackers do that? Is that why she was kidnapped? It all seemed ludicrous, but she was here.

She licked her dry lips, moaning, as they half dragged, half carried her into the midst of a woodland clearing, ringed by dilapidated buildings made of logs and stones. It looked like a scene out of one of the Highland historical romances she loved to read, except that she'd seen the computer. Throngs of men, some in kilts and others in breeches, made their way to a barn-like structure set at the edge of the compound.

"Let me go..." she started to say but it only came out as a mumble. Whatever they'd given her, she was still high on it and felt strangely disconnected from her body.

"Good, she's coming out of it," Kill said, stepping in front of the men supporting her dead weight to leer at her. "We'll take her to my cabin."

She averted his gaze, not wanting to give him the satisfaction of scaring her, sensing her fear would make him gloat. She'd kick his rank ass the minute she was free, she promised herself. He stepped in front of her to trap her face in a painful grip so that she couldn't look away.

"Open your eyes, Princess, and see who you belong to."

She glared at him knowing he saw her disgust when he snarled. "I belong to myself, and no one else, you smelly bastard." She heard the men holding their chuckle, watched Kill's face redden with rage, and bit her tongue at her rash words. She had to be smart and survive, until Lucas could rescue her, and taunting her captor wasn't smart. She had no doubt that Lucas would come for her. She just had to bide her time.

Kill's smile was cruel. "Just as I thought, the bastard's cock wasn't enough to train her. No wonder he tried to refuse the breeding barns."

Breeding barns? Her gaze fell on a barn-like structure the men had gone into. Through the open double doors she saw dozens of naked men and women housed inside. Two women on all fours were being fucked. Appalled, Charity couldn't look away, just as aware of the curious stares coming her way from those inside the breeding barn. The men gave her a hungry once over. The women looked curious and angry.

"Look well, lass, at your proper place in this society," Kill said, his grip tightening. "You'll be my breed bitch, and if you please me, my first wife." He tugged at her bodice, tearing the front of her dress in two, the buttons giving way, and there was a cry of approval from the men.

"No," she cried, trying to kick him, but he jumped back out of range like the coward he was.

"Get her inside before Rowan gets back," he said with a growl.

The men dragged her into a small stone building containing a rush bed with a tartan atop it, and a roughhewn table and chairs. They forced her up against one of the thick stone walls, pinioning her to it. Damp cold seeped through what was left of her sundress. She glared at Kill when he followed them inside with a smirk. He was crazy. He was also aroused, judging by the bulge in his pants.

"Let her go, curs, and learn well how to bring an Elite bitch to heel." He lifted a thick leather strap from a hook on the wall. "The princess is going to grace us with a performance."

What was all this princess crap? Garth, and even Lucas, had referred to her that way. And now she realized it was more than just a snipe at her privileged upbringing. These people actually thought she was royalty. Oh god, when they learned the truth, she was so dead. The men let her go and she cried out in pain as the blood rushed back into her arms. Kill laughed out loud and she glared at him. He obviously wasn't playing with a full deck. Was he going to try to tie her up with the strap? He flicked the strap at her, catching her thighs, and she cried out in shock and pain.

"Show us how an Elite bitch pleasures herself," Kill said with a grin.

Charity stood there frozen, appalled, her thighs throbbing in pain. But there was no way she'd give in to his sick demand. "No." The strap caught her on her abdomen. She wrapped her arms protectively around herself.

"Or would you rather take it in the mating barn?"

She glared back at the mocking, glaring beast, and then remembered the women she'd seen being used in the barn. Oh god, he meant it. She couldn't and there was only one way to mollify him for now. She slowly caressed her abdomen, her skin bared by her ripped clothing. Kill and his minion's leers made her shudder and close her eyes, thinking of Lucas. He always seemed to read her thoughts, know when she needed him. Where was he now? Kill's hands were on her then, pushing hers aside, his rough fingers pinching her breasts, slipping between her legs.

"Wait until I'm buried deep inside you, bitch, you'll forget all about that limp dicked bastard wolf."

"Never," she spat. "You don't have what it takes to satisfy me."

Kill's face turned red with rage before he slapped her, sending her crashing to the floor. He fell on her, pawing at her as she kicked and bit at him.

"That's the way, Kill, show that Elite bitch how we Betas mate."

"They like to be played with first," the other one said.

"What the hell's going on here," a deep voice bellowed.

Kill stilled on top of her and bit out a vicious curse. He rolled off her, springing to his feet, and she sat up, looking gratefully at the older man who'd walked in, saving her. Big, powerful, barbaric; he carried that aura. He was wearing leather breeches and wore a plaid over his shoulder. His spooky blue eyes reminded her of Kill's, but his handsome features reminded her of Lucas. This had to be Rowan, the biological father they shared.

"I'm just teaching the Elite bitch her place, sire," Kill said.

The old man's scowl made Kill fall silent and bow.

"You stupid whelp brat. I didn't give orders for her to be taken yet. I won't let you fuck this one up like you did her sister. Go outside while I interrogate the princess."

"Why do you idiots keep calling me that?" She scowled up at them as they turned to look at her. Instead of answering, they both stared at her exposed breasts, their leers turning to shocked glares.

"She bears his mark," Kill said.

The old man scowled. "They've mated, but they haven't bound. Look, even now his mark fades."

They were back to talking about her as if she wasn't there and it pissed her off.

"Mated?" she asked looking down at what she'd assumed was a hickey. The heart-shaped mark was a little bit faded she realized. But a mating mark, what the heck did that mean? "But I don't under..."

Rowan grinned. "You bear Lucas's mating mark, but have no fear, Kill will soon knock it out of you. By the light of the blue moon, Kill will take you, and mate with you and take his rightful place in the pack." He looked at Kill. "Secure her so we can go to the auction. We have to make an appearance."

Charity struggled as Kill locked her in manacles attached to the wall. She glared up at Rowan who watched with approval.

The old man cackled. "Chip off the old block, this one."

"Yeah, rotten to the core," she commented.

He cast a startled look her way then roared with laughter. "You may be right at that, Princess, but being brutal has kept our clan alive for centuries."

Chapter 8

Lucas paced outside Charity's locked bedroom door. It would have been easy for him to open, but he didn't want to invade her privacy.

"We're ready, Lobo," Garth said, coming into Lucas's hotel room.

Lucas couldn't stop the fierce glare he gave him.

"Whoa, don't kill the messenger. We can take another flight."

"Sorry, I'll hurry Charity." *That is, if she's even still speaking to me.* He was stepping toward her door when the smell hit him. Betas, their faint foul odor, masked by something else...Charity's perfume. "Damn it all." He reached for the door to find it locked, and then willed it to open for him. The tumblers turned in the latch and he pulled it wide open. Charity was gone, her open suitcase on the bed, her spilled perfume running off the dresser to the carpet below.

"Betas," Garth said with a growl.

Lucas turned to see his pal sniff the air as Bran zapped into the room. "Come on, we don't have much time."

He tore open a time portal and they transported to the Beta encampment. Lucas crouched in the bushes; Garth and Bran crouched beside him in wolf form. Rowan, Kill, and two other males headed out to the mating barn for the auction. Their voices carried, telling him he'd come just in time. Kill was to mate with Charity at midnight, and then wait to take him out in an ambush. They knew he'd come despite their efforts to mask her scent, but they hadn't counted on him coming this quickly. Luckily, they didn't know half his powers.

A sound from the mating barn made him spin in that direction. The auction had started. Betas from all the packs would be here to purchase breeding bitches. It meant a huge night's profit for Rowan, one he couldn't pass up for a princess. Lucas sensed that was the reason Kill chose to snatch Charity tonight. He'd always chafed under the old wolf's command. Rowan would dangle Charity over Kill's head as a prize for being a good boy. He sneered, wanting nothing more than to gut the two of them, but vengeance would have to come later. Right now, he had to find her.

Lucas pointed toward the cabins, motioning for them to check the outer cabins first. Garth nodded, ran toward Rowan's cabin, and peered inside. His plaid was flung across his bed, a wolf's skin, Rowan's emblem of chiefdom hung on the wall.

He passed on to the next dwelling. A lone figure was curled up on a bench in the corner. As he moved, Lucas saw that it was one of Rowan's sons, the one they kept hidden. Why was he held prisoner? Lucas couldn't risk asking him, for fear of him giving them away. He ground his teeth in frustration, hating to see any man caged, and headed for the next cabin.

He searched two more cabins before he came across the third. Charity was manacled to the wall. His gut clenched when he saw her sagged against the wall, her dress torn, tears staining her cheeks. He transported inside with Garth and Bran still in wolf form beside him.

"Baby, I'm so sorry those wolves hurt you," he said, falling to his knees beside her. He pulled the manacles out of the wall with shaking hands, and took Charity in his arms.

"I knew you'd come," she said, kissing his jaw.

Her eyes widened as she pulled back to look from the empty manacles to him and then took in his wolf companions. Without a word, he picked her up and teleported them back to their suite in the Flamingo.

*****

Charity was trembling, numb, as she stood in the middle of the room. The stagnant scent of Kill and her perfume made her gag. Her shocked gaze took in the wolves that in an instant turned into Bran and Garth inside her living room. Good heavens, Garth was nude. Her eyes widened as she stared at his package. He had nothing on Lucas.

"Cover it up, will ya, before we all go blind," Lucas muttered, seeing the direction of her stare.

Her eyes widened as Garth turned beet red and clothes suddenly covered his nudity. Had she seen what she'd thought she'd seen? Garth and Bran turned from wolves to people? Even though it seemed impossible, it all came together in her mind. She'd seen those wolves before. They were two of the wolves she'd seen fighting. A larger timber wolf had helped them. Lucas. She turned to stare at him, noting too late that the brown eyes matched. Lucas was the big timber she'd saved. He was half wolf? And then there was the change in herself she'd felt when they were making love. Was it even possible she had powers, too, that she was a wolf? There was also the issue of the strange mark on her breast. Going by Rowan's angry words, it was a mating mark.

It all seemed impossible, a fairy tale gone wrong, except she was living it. The fact that Lucas had picked her up and they'd all suddenly popped into her living room couldn't be denied. She looked at his chest. Was he marked under his shirt? She had to know. "Let me see it." He opened his shirt to show the matching mating mark. It was true. "Then this means..."

"Now sweetheart, don't be scared."

She frowned, as clothes somehow materialized on her, replacing her torn dress. "I'm not scared, I'm bloody furious. How dare you manipulate me like this? Who put you up to it?" At his wary look, she heard the word "Princess" replaying through her mind. It meant her dad had to be the king. What kind of craziness was this? "My dad put you up to this didn't he?"

Lucas looked over his shoulder at Bran and Garth. "Uh, you want to give us a moment, guys."

"You're going with them," she said, marching him toward the door.

"No. I'm not going anywhere. In case you forgot, you're in extreme danger here." He turned to Garth and Brad. "Pack us up, boys, and get us on the next flight out of here. We're leaving."

"Think again. I'm not going anywhere with you." At his sad look, she felt guilty. "I need my time, and my space to think. You can guard me from afar. I'll have three big, strong...whatever you are..." She looked at him for clarification.

"Werewolves," he filled in.

She braced herself, already guessing the answer. "Fine, I'll have you werewolves to look after me. And why fly? Why don't you just beam us home?"

"You're not ready for that." At her glare he let out a sigh, grasped her hand, and teleported them.

She wasn't surprised to see Garth stark naked again or standing in her living room. Instead, she was numb.

"I'll give you some privacy." Lucas turned to leave. He hesitated a moment by the door, then followed the others out.

"I'll scream if I need you."

"Don't bother, I'm telepathic, I can read your mind."

She slammed and locked the door. Great. Who needed a guy who could read her thoughts?

She did, she thought forlornly, and snatched up the phone. "Chas, I'm home from Vegas and I need some answers fast. Just what am I?" The silence on the other end of the line told her.

"Um. What's the matter, Chari? Is Lucas there with you?"

"Any reason why he should be?" She couldn't help baiting her evasive sister. She'd known for months that Chas was hiding something.

"Well...I mean you've just come back from Vegas and I'd figured you'd, um...well Justin and I didn't wait."

The arranged marriage part was true too. She felt like crying. "Oh no," she whimpered into the phone.

"Are you hurt?"

"Define hurt," she said, collapsing on the sofa.

"Sit tight, I'll be there in a flash with reinforcements."

Charity sat there, staring into space, waiting for Chas to materialize out of thin air.

*****

Lucas stood rigidly outside Charity's door. As expected, she'd rejected him, so why did it hurt so damned much? It made the formality of binding with him a moot point. It was never going to happen, and he'd been a lovesick fool to think it ever could. Still, he had a job to finish. Until the Blue Moon was past, he'd stay by Charity, whether she wanted him or not. Garth and Bran were in position outside the building, within shouting distance, if he should need them.

At least Charity had the presence of mind to call her sister for help, a calm move considering all she'd been through. His woman made him proud. It saved him from breaking focus to call in the Elite for backup to give her extra personal protection. Chastity and Justin flashed in right on schedule. Lucas braced himself; Chastity's glare was enough to freeze his balls off.

Justin leaned against a wall giving him a casual nod. "Lobo."

Lucas inclined his head. "Justin."

"What in the hell did you do to my sister?" Chastity demanded.

Lucas took a half step back, surprised by her fire. They'd done each other all right, but he wasn't the kind to kiss and tell. He didn't miss Justin's rueful smile.

"This isn't the time," Lucas said.

"Like hell it isn't, I—"

"He's right, honey," Justin cut in gently but firmly, and then turned to Lucas. "There was trouble?"

"Kill and a hunting party kidnapped Charity, took her to Rowan's hunting cabin in the Brey Forest. I got her back when they went to the mating barn auction, end of story."

"Not quite," Justin said, looking pointedly at Lucas's chest.

Lucas pulled open the collar of his shirt, showing them the mating mark above his left nipple, knowing he could be signing his death warrant with the Elite. Charles Langford would probably gut him; maybe it would be better than a life spent alone and sexless. He glanced from Justin's grim look to Chastity's wide eyes.

"But she said you two didn't do it." She clasped a hand over her mouth. "Oops."

"Why don't you go see your sister. Lucas and I have things to talk over." Justin handed her a talisman. "Use this to go to the bunker. I want you both out of the line of fire."

Lucas nodded. At least Charity would be safe. Seeing her safe was all that counted anymore. He braced himself as Charity opened the door to admit her sister. The angry look Charity shot him made him shrink inside. She let Chastity in and shut the door in his face, blocking him out.

His spine rigid, he turned to face Justin, prepared for annihilation.

"You have back up?" Justin asked.

Lucas nodded. The question took him by surprise. He'd thought there'd be hell to pay for touching a Blue Moon Princess early. "Yeah, flanking the house, why?"

"They'll hit again."

"Tell me something I don't know." Lucas watched the barb roll off the roguish Elite male and sighed, relenting. "The blue moon is two nights away. They're going to go ape shit when they find her gone and come after her with all they have."

"Succinctly put," Justin said with an icy smile. "Where do you want me?"

Touched, Lucas nonetheless raised a brow. "Buddy, I'm not that kind of wolf."

"Cute."

"You can help me most by being a liaison with her father. Make sure she's okay and gets to choose her own mate next time around."

*****

Charity walked back to the sofa, Chas following behind her. Lucas, the hunky werewolf outside her door, was practically calling out to her, and damn she wanted to answer. She could feel his vibrations, sense him, damned near taste him. Fighting the feeling, she sagged down onto the sofa, and curled up into a ball, casting a baleful look at her sister, looking for signs of change. "You don't look like a werewolf, Chas."

Chas rolled her eyes. "Neither do you, Chari, and we prefer the term were-folk or Wolfen."

"It's true then." Chas's mouth clapped shut and, a moment later, Chas nodded. Charity had always sensed there was something different about her family, but this, it was so preposterous.

"It's true. We're werewolves of the Elite clan. All of us but Momma, that is, who's human, and Clari, who's something else. It seems she's a throwback to another time."

"How do you know all this?" Chas was standing there discussing it like it was normal. How could she be so nonchalant, unless she'd always known? That had to be it. Maybe her parents didn't think she was mature enough to handle it. That hurt. "Why didn't they tell me? Why was I kept in the dark about all this?"

"Don't feel so all alone. I didn't find out until Justin and I were about to be mated. In short, our parents kept us in the dark to protect us from the big bad wolf."

Charity thought of Rowan and shuddered. "I think I've met him."

"Now isn't the time to muddle this out. You've got bigger problems. Unless, maybe you don't bear the Alpha's mating mark."

Chari felt her sister's curious gaze on her and hesitated, then reluctantly tugged open the neckline of her blouse to show the mark. She gazed down at the entwined hearts on the upper curve of her breast, noting the raised pattern. It was beautiful, actually, and very scary.

"You do," Chas said with a gasp. "I hadn't thought it possible."

Hadn't thought it possible? She and Lucas were dynamite together, when he wasn't turning into a wolf, and maybe even better when he was. "Gee thanks, I do know how to have sex, thank you very much."

"Poor Lucas."

She surged off the couch. "What do you mean 'poor Lucas?' Sleeping with me isn't a fate worse than death."

"Maybe not for you. When you don't bind with him, your mark will fade and you can move on to another. True, it won't be a love match and the sex won't be satisfying. Lucas, on the other hand, will bear the mark forever and never mate with another. He'll be alone."

"A lone wolf, what a cliché."

"Wait, it gets worse. Eventually, he'll be emasculated, losing even his desire and ability for sex."

Chari blinked up at her in shock. Lucas essentially gelded. It couldn't be. He was so virile. "So help me, Chas, if you're making this up I'm going to kill you."

Chas showed her own mating mark, a star-shaped emblem on her forehead. "I'm not. Our marks are distinctive and aren't visible to humans. Most couples don't even get mating marks. If they do it means they're fated to be together, and it's permanent. Unfortunately, even Mother Nature sometimes makes mistakes."

"Lucas is not a mistake." Charity prayed it wasn't a lie. The sexual and emotional attraction between them was deep. So deep that she knew she could never let him go.

"Of course he's not, sis," Chas said walking up to her. "Now how about we get the hell out of Dodge before the shooting starts."

Chapter 9

"Shooting?" Chari frowned, jumping to her feet. A thud out in the hall accompanied by a familiar stench made the fine hair on her nape stand on end. It was the smell of the Betas who'd kidnapped her.

"Okay, biting and maiming then." Chas grabbed her hand.

"No," Chari cried in frustration as she felt herself dematerialize and watched her sister go transparent. Suddenly they were in her father's office. Her parents and Clarity stood there waiting. Charity took in their worried expressions. Her mother's eyes were red-rimmed and her father's scowl was fierce. Now his tendency to growl made sense. He was the picture of an outraged werewolf.

Light beams hit a painting on the wall behind his desk, snagging her attention. Funny she'd never noticed how beautiful it was before. Maybe the fact that it portrayed a wolf made her identify with it. Her father's hand on her arm broke the spell. She looked up at him, noticing he was staring at her mating mark, his face turning red with anger.

Clarity stepped forward, gaining Charles's attention. "They're in trouble, Dad."

"I ought to geld the impudent whelp," he said under his breath. He turned to Joanna. "Get her into the bunker before the light on the painting tempts her away from us."

"Wait, Daddy," Charity wailed, but her father was already striding from the room. Her dad wouldn't really hurt Lucas for sleeping with her, would he? And what did Clarity mean by trouble? He didn't even break his stride. Her mother pushed a button on a control panel, and the back wall whisked silently open. Clari and Chas closed ranks behind Charity, herding her inside.

"Stop pushing," she snapped. She hadn't even known this bunker existed. A quick glance around told her they could hold up for an extended siege. What kind of trouble were they expecting? Picturing Rowan's and Kill's flinty eyes, she knew. She dug in her heels, standing her ground. "Mom, we've got to come up with a plan to rescue my mate." Her mom's frown didn't give her hope. Her sisters exchanged a worried glance.

"It's probably Stockholm Syndrome making her say that," Clari said to Chas.

"No, it's true. They did the dirty," Chas whispered back.

Joanna gave them both a quelling look. "Girl's, let's try to maintain a little decorum." She turned back to Charity with a sigh. "I'm sorry, honey, but we can't interfere. Besides, you'd distract him, likely make things worse."

"Yeah, and he's got his hands full even with his friends helping him. I can sense it. I only hope that Dad and Justin get there in time," Clari said.

Chas rolled her eyes. "Lay off the woo woo psychic stuff will ya, sis? You're scaring Char. We've got to talk some sense into her, Mom. She thinks that barbarian Alpha is her true-lifemate. It's impossible."

"Who's to say what's impossible? I'm human and your father and I are mated." Joanna put a comforting arm around Charity and led her to the table.

"Why do they keep calling him an Alpha?" Charity asked. "Teach me about this so I can understand."

"Our Wolfen society is broken down into three divisions: Elite, more human than wolf; Betas, more wolf than human; and Alphas, half-breeds like Lucas. They're considered dangerously unstable."

Charity shook her head. "He's not, he's very controlled." *Even down to his cyber seduction of me.* "Is it true? This was only a job for him?"

"Not a job, a promise fulfilled. You were promised to Lucas's half-brother, Lash, when you were born. Lash was killed rescuing Lucas from his Beta captors, and Lucas honored his dying request to take his place as your mate."

*****

Lucas smelled trouble. It smelled like Beta breath. He popped into Charity's flat in time to see two Betas come though the patio door. In an instant, he was on them.

They turned and ran. He gave chase. The stabbing pain in his back came as a surprise. He snarled and turned to see Kill behind him, dagger in hand. An ambush, how could he be so recklessly stupid? Love. It was turning him into a fool and making him careless.

Feeling his strength deplete, he vowed to take them all down with him and turned on Kill with a snarl. As more Betas closed on him, he heard a new battle cry. A quick, startled glance told him that Justin and Charles Langford were wading into the fray alongside his Alpha friends. Getting a second wind, he dispatched the first Beta and then looked for Kill in time to see him vanish. Damn him for an opportunistic coward.

Then Langford went down as a Beta jumped him from behind. Lucas growled, sending the Beta flying and then used his powers to tear open a time portal and send the attacker hurtling back into time. The stinky bastard went with a startled cry on his lips and the others soon followed. Lucas gave Langford a hand up. "Now what's this I hear about gelding me?" he asked Charles, then wobbled on his feet.

Bran and Garth caught Lucas and eased him down on the sofa. Bran pulled off Lucas's shirt to reveal two stab wounds in his back and his mating mark. Hissing at the burn as Bran started the healing process, Lucas glanced up at Charles Langford's narrowed eyes.

*****

Annoyed by Chastity's continued dismissal of Lucas as a proper mate for an Elite, Charity glared back at her and rubbed her sore leg. Something was poking her leg. She hitched up her skirt to rub the irritated bump.

"What's wrong, did the bastard give you fleas?" Chas asked.

"Not funny," Charity said, pulling up her skirt to reveal a red spot on her thigh.

"Oh my God, they tagged her," Clari said.

"Tagged as in bugged?" Charity stared at the red spot, seeing the tiny sliver of metal sticking out of her skin.

Joanna gently pulled the sliver out of Charity's leg, and then threw it in the trash. "Don't worry, girls. The thick walls should protect—"

They all smelled it at the same time—smoke and Beta stench. "Oh no, I led them to us."

Joanna scowled at the sealed door. Wisps of smoke curled underneath it. "How dare they presume to break the covenant this way? At least there aren't any employees around to get caught in the crossfire." She turned to the girls. "Remain calm, girls. Charity, go and get towels to absorb the smoke. Chastity, go to the cabinet and get the guns. Clarity, try to make contact with your father."

"Yes, Mom," they all parroted back. Charity placed the rolled towels under the door's crack, blocking the smoke, just as something crashed against it. Yelping, she tumbled back on her butt, then jumped up and ran back to the table. She gaped at her mom who was hefting a shotgun.

"You can't kill a werewolf, can you? Unless that thing's packed with silver bullets. Right?" Charity asked hoping for everyone's said she was right. "At least that's what I've seen in the movies."

*****

Lucas winced as Bran cauterized his stab wound. He glanced up at Justin and Charles Langford as they talked. Langford turned to look at him then.

"How'd you do that?"

"Do what?"

"Tear open a time portal? Send them packing?"

Lucas shrugged. "I'm a freak. It goes with the territory."

"I never quite saw anything like it." Langford stopped talking and frowned.

Pain stabbed Lucas in his head a second before he heard Charity's voice in his mind.

"They're under siege," Lucas and Charles said at the same time.

Lucas surged to his feet. He wobbled a bit but braced himself, meeting Charles's worried glance with one of his own. No matter the cost, they had women to protect.

They transported to Langford and Langford. Lucas, Charles, Justin, Bran, and a naked Garth touched down in Charles's office waiting room. Wisps of smoke curled the air, but Lucas didn't detect any active fire. He zapped clothes on Garth, and they rushed into Charles's office and toward the bunker. The bunker door was open, the doorway smoldering. Charity and Chastity, both in wolf form, held down a wailing Beta. Charity growled, lying flat on the back of one Beta, nipping at his flailing hands. Chastity tackled another, taking him to ground with a growl.

"Look out, sis," Clarity said, aiming a blast of the fire extinguisher at first one and then the other. They howled, cowering in submission, while Kill stood snarling in the corner.

"Make one move and you're dead," Joanna said, holding a gun on Kill. She swore when he vanished. "And don't come back or you'll be picking silver buckshot out of your ass," Joanna yelled after him.

The men shared an amused look.

"I see the ladies have this well in hand." Charles took the shotgun from his wife and laid it on the table. He pulled her into his arms. "You were magnificent, dear."

Clarity gave the Beta one last squirt as Charity and Chastity turned back into human form.

"Doesn't leave a man much left to do," commented Justin, pulling Chastity into his embrace.

"Too true," Lucas said, sending the whimpering Beta back to where he came. "Hardly gives a guy an opportunity to be a hero." He turned to look at Charity, gauging her reaction. Her troubled frown made his heart sink.

"Daddy, don't you dare geld him. He's my mate and I'm keeping him."

Lucas caught Charity as she launched herself at him. Hope warmed his whole being. He felt his mating mark intensify. Hugging her, he glanced over her shoulder at her parents.

Charles glanced down at his wife and chuckled. "We sure raised some feisty, independent princesses."

Joanna smiled. "Despite all your growling you wouldn't have it any other way, would you, dear?"

"You're right, my dear," Charles agreed then turned to rake Lucas and Charity's embrace with a satisfied glance. "Hell, honey, you can keep him. It takes a hell of a wolf to stand up to the Betas. You two have my blessings."

Lucas looked deep into his mate's shining, violet eyes. "Will you bind with me, Charity?"

"I wouldn't have it any other way, my laird," she said, pulling him down for a kiss.

Joanna beamed at the happy couple and then turned to her other daughters. "It looks like we've got a last minute wedding to plan, girls."

Clarity turned to her father. "I think the invitations are already out, aren't they, Dad?"

Charles flushed at the startled look from his wife. "I had a feeling," he said with a shrug.

Joanna nodded. "I guess I should be used to your fey ways by now husband. You could have told me."

"I didn't want to jinx it. I did leave all the girly details to you."

Clarity grinned. "It's about time you came clean, Dad, now maybe everything will get back to normal around here. I've got the flowers covered, my garden has an abundance of blooms."

"I wouldn't count on things settling down," Chastity said, and then smiled ruefully. "I wouldn't have picked him for her, but she loves him, so maybe Father does know best. I'll take care of the music."

Joanna smiled. "Thanks, girls, all that's left is the cake and dress, and I can see to them. I'll give the chef and dressmaker orders to commence."

Chapter 10

Charity stood at the entrance to Langford and Langford's courtyard under the magical light of the blue moon. Members of the extended Elite clan gathered in the garden for the binding ceremony along with Lucas's Alpha clan. It was a historic moment for the two segments of wolf society to socialize together. True peace had yet to be achieved with the Betas, but now wasn't the time to worry about that. It was a time to rejoice.

Justin, Lucas's best man, wearing a black tuxedo, walked up to a flower-strewn arbor. Bran and Garth followed him dressed in formal Scottish kilts, as was the Alpha way. Charity bit back a small grin thinking of her fantasizing about men in kilts. Then Lucas walked up to the head of the aisle, and took her breath away. His plaid, of red, green, and gold was one she'd never seen before, and he looked drop dead gorgeous in it. His bare chest glistening in the candlelight showed his mating mark, his strong, hair-covered thighs sticking out of his kilt made her wonder if he wore anything underneath.

As a guitar and lute began playing, Chastity walked down the aisle carrying a bouquet of hydrangeas that matched her tea-length blue silk gown beaded with pearls. A sapphire-studded tiara glistened in her hair. She flashed Justin a secret smile as she took her place across from him.

Clarity, holding a bouquet of lilacs that matched her tea-length gown sewn through with crystals, wore a tiara studded with amethysts. She gave Bran's kilt a playful glance as she neared him.

A bagpiper joined the guitarist and lute. Charity drew in a deep breath and took her father's arm, her bouquet of white roses and heather trembling a little in her hand. The wedding guests stood and turned to look at her. She heard their pleased murmurs and felt like the princess they thought she was. Her long white gown had a low sweetheart neckline displaying her mating mark, and her ruby-studded tiara felt like a crown. She'd been shocked when her mother had put the gem-studded crown on her head.

She only had eyes for Lucas as her father escorted her down the aisle and toward her destiny. Lucas was so handsome and seemed a bit nervous as he waited for her at the altar. When she gazed into his eyes all else faded away. He was her lifemate.

Two ministers stepped up to the altar, the Elite Parson Eliot in white robes, the Alpha Chaplain Wolfe in breeches and plaid.

Parson Eliot began. "All assembled, we joyfully gather together to celebrate a wedding."

Chaplain Wolfe nodded. "We also celebrate the joining of our two Wolfen packs. May this be the start of a new harmony between our kinds."

Parson Eliot looked down at Charity and Lucas. "A thousand welcomes to you and your bride, Lucas Kendal. May you be healthy all your days. May you be blessed with long life and peace. May you grow old with goodness and with riches." He looked out at the wedding guests. "Is there any objection from either clan to this match?"

Charity froze, worried someone might object. She turned to give the guests a forbidding scowl, and they erupted in laughter. Not very princess-like, but she got her point across.

Lucas took her hand turning her around. "Easy, honey."

"There is no objection," Charles Langford said. "I, her mother, and our people freely give my middle daughter Charity to bind to his Alpha clan."

Charity looked at her father then, all the love and admiration she had for him welling up inside her. Her dad leaned over and kissed her cheek.

"Be happy," he said, before placing her hand in Lucas's.

Her father tied a red ribbon around their joined hands. "This red ribbon symbolizes strength and the abiding passion between bind-mates."

Joanna smiled and tied a purple ribbon around their joined hands. "This ribbon stands for love and harmony."

Chaplain Wolfe smiled. "And now for the Alpha part of the ceremony. The plaid please."

Garth handed him the folded plaid. The minister blessed it and handed it to Lucas.

"Charity, my love, do you accept my plaid, my clan as your own? Will you bind with me for all the days of our lives?"

Tears of joy misted Charity's eyes. She nodded. "Lucas, I accept your plaid, your clan as my own." Charity stood still as Lucas gently draped his family's red, green, and gold plaid over her shoulders. Then he took a Celtic wedding ring from Justin and placed it on her finger.

She took the larger Celtic band that Chastity held and turned to Lucas. "Lucas, will you bind with me? Will you take this ring as a symbol of our abiding love?"

"Charity, honey, I will bind with you, and wear your ring as a symbol of my love for you."

Both clergymen smiled saying, "We now pronounce you husband and wife. What has been brought together this evening, let no creature put asunder."

Lucas scooped Charity up in his arms. Charity laughed and tossed her bouquet in the general direction of the guests and saw Clarity catch it. "You're next," she shouted over her groom's shoulder.

"Not bloody likely," Clarity shouted back and handed the bouquet off to another woman.

"Decorum," her mother shushed.

As Lucas carried her off to their mating chamber, "Wild Thing" blared forth from the amplifiers. Her pointed look at a laughing Chastity told her who the culprit was. Her mom gave up trying for decorum as the guests started dancing in the aisles.

"Look," Charity said when she saw her mom and Garth dancing.

"Well I'll be. I wouldn't have believed it myself."

*****

Lucas didn't slow down until he had them in their mating chamber. He'd stolen a princess's heart and he wasn't giving her up. He bolted the door and then set her down, gazing at her in wonder. He could still hardly believe it, that this vision of loveliness wanted him.

"Come here, mate," Charity said, quirking a finger at him.

Lucas stepped toward her, suddenly feeling unprepared. Mating he knew, binding was another story. He pulled Charity into his arms and kissed her. She kissed him back melting into his embrace. Her stiff nipples rubbing against him through her gown drove him crazy. Lucas touched her gown and it fell off her so that she was suddenly naked, shivering with excitement in his arms.

"You've got to teach me how to do that," she said, stepping out of her gown.

"All in good time, honey," he said, picking her up and carrying her to bed. "You've got a lifetime to learn all my tricks." She nibbled on his ear and he hissed with pleasure.

"Sounds delightful, but you're wearing too many clothes, Mr. Kendal."

Lucas let out a teasing growl when she reached down to cup his growing erection under the kilt.

"Kilt be gone," she murmured and then sighed. "Maybe I don't have any powers after all."

He laughed, his kilt disappearing. He picked her up and laid her onto the bed, coming down on top of her to press her into the mattress. His stiff cock rubbed tantalizingly against her warm thigh, killing him with the urgency to be inside her. "Honey, you've got all the powers you'll ever need."

Charity smiled, opening her legs. "Take me, my husband and lifemate."

Lucas settled against her warm, welcoming body, her pussy wetting the head of his cock. "Your wish is my command, wife." He looked down at her. "Ready?" He didn't miss the sudden, expressive longing in her big, violet eyes.

"Yes."

He took her hand. "Our hands are bound, our bodies joined as one," he said in a low rumble, surging into her. "I take you as my one true mate, Charity."

Charity moaned, her pussy clutching to his cock as her body and soul claimed him as her own. "Our hands are bound, our bodies joined," she moaned, wrapping her legs around him as he took her to orgasm. "I take you as my one true mate, Lucas, my laird."

A cheer went up from the crowd in the courtyard as their binding symbol glowed in the night sky.

Award-winning author **Honey Jans** is a natural born romantic. In her life she's worn many hats, from wife to mother, and caregiver to salesperson. They've all combined to make her who she is: a writer who weaves together tales of love, from the sweet to the decidedly erotic. She lives in scenic central Wisconsin with her husband, but loves to travel to exotic locales. She belongs to RWA, WisRWA, Desert Rose, and PAN, and EPIC, and writes for various publishers as well as for her own personal satisfaction. You can find her hanging out online at www.honeyjans.com, http://honeyjanserotica.blogspot.com. Honey loves hearing from her readers at eggbert@charter.net.

Once In Love With Laura
Blue Ribbon Rating: 5!
"***ONCE IN LOVE WITH LAURA*** is one of those stories that 'speaks' to you through the characters' emotional attachment for each other. With plenty of smoldering sex scenes, comical and witty dialogue, and an element of suspense, I happily sat and read this story straight through. I especially loved Laura's reaction to Nick's dominant demeanor. Laura and Nick make a wonderful couple, and as you read their story, you can't help but admire them. Honey Jans tells wonderful BDSM tales and seems to be improving her talent at her craft with each new story."
Reviewed by: Chrissy Dionne • Romance Junkies

Cindy Revisited
4 ½ Blue Ribbons!
"Honey Jans takes a much beloved fairy tale and puts a modern spin on it with delightful results in her newest release ***CINDY REVISITED***. I admit that I loved the fairy tale Cinderella, but I enjoyed this story even more because rather than being sugary sweet, the plot is sexy, wicked, and far more realistic than the Disney version. There may not be a fairy godmother in real life, but sometimes extraordinary things happen and you know—there's nothing wrong with dreaming

about finding a special man ready, willing, and able to whisk us away from the doldrums of life. This is a fun, imaginative tale with a bit of suspense which I'm sure readers will thoroughly enjoy."

Reviewed by: Chrissy Dionne • Romance Junkies

Monica's Manhunt
Blue Ribbon Rating: 5!
"***MONICA'S MANHUNT*** by Honey Jans is the long awaited sequel to APRIL LOVE. Ms. Jans, in my opinion, can be considered the 'Mistress of Eroticism.' She draws you into her books like no other. Everything is so realistic and her story blends together with the characters making you wish it never had to end! I highly recommend reading ***MONICA'S MANHUNT*** along with the other books by Ms. Jans. You won't be sorry you did!"

Reviewed by: Connie Spears • Romance Junkies

A Wolf's Tale
5 Cups!
"You will never think of Little Red Riding Hood the same after you read *A Wolf's Tale*. Ms. Jans has created her own exceptionally hot version and loaded it with plenty of twists and turns. Mitchell is one sexy alpha male; what woman would not want to come across a wolf like Mitchell? Then you have Gina, a woman who is headstrong and independent, with a love for wolves. Mix all of these characters with the twists and turns, add some really sizzling hot sex, and you have a fairy tale you wish would come true."

Reviewed by: Wateena • Coffee Time Romance

The Commanders Club
4 Stars!
"Another winner from an author whose name is becoming synonymous with words like tempestuous and ecstasy. The latest journey into the world of dominant men and the women

they control is thrilling and stormy and stimulates the reader into a deep longing that screams to be fulfilled. I look forward to whatever this author has next since she's shown in the past that she has what it takes to weave stories that leave readers panting for more."

Reviewed by: Rachelle • Enchanted In Romance

April Love
5 Cups!
"HONEY JANS writes a book that will keep you up until all hours of the night. This book is so hot, you will need ice water to cool down. It's a keeper."

Reviewed by: Sherry • Coffee Time Romance

Awards:
2006 ~ EPIC eBook award for Best Anthology of the Year for TALES OF THE TREASURE TROVE, a Jewels of the Quill Anthology

You can find more on **Honey Jans** and her books at:

Her Website
www.honeyjans.com

Her Blog
http://honeyjanserotica.blogspot.com
Follow her on Facebook
https://www.facebook.com/HoneyJansStreetTeam

A Sneak Peek

Never in A Blue Moon
By
Shari Dare

Book 3
Blue Moon Magic

Coming
February 2015

Unwilling to admit to the fact the Blue Moon held any meaning for her, Clarity Langford is surprised when Tom Morrison left his mating mark on her. But would her life go as expected or would Rowan try to ruin things for her?

Clarity Langford couldn't understand her sisters. They acted the way she did when she first went to college and was out from under her father's thumb. James Farnsworth, her first lover, had loved her and dumped her. Once awakened, she found sex exciting. Of course, it was still exciting, but it certainly didn't consume her every waking moment the way it did her sisters. As the corporate accountant, she'd learned to balance business and pleasure.

The way Chas and Char behaved, anyone would think they were horny teenagers rather than thirty-something married women. After they'd mated, she'd thought their bad behavior would end. Instead, they were so intent on a good fuck, it was almost frightening. They knew who and what they were now, so identity confusion was no excuse. Of course, finding out you were a werewolf could be upsetting. Clarity had known of the differences in the three sisters for years. She'd been a sophomore in college when their mother explained that she was one hundred percent human while her sisters were Wolfen. It was a secret her mother only told her, because her sisters were not to be told until they came into heat.

They had just recently come into heat, but that didn't excuse their behavior in her book. The difference made her life shorter, and therefore she'd found sexual pleasure earlier.

"What's up, Clarity?" Tom Morrison asked as he entered the office.

Just the sound of his voice made her pussy lips weep. He'd been hot as a pistol last night when they played sex games in her apartment.

"Not much," she replied. "It's just this P & L statement has me bugged." *And my clit is throbbing like Ricky Ricardo's conga drum.* If she were like Chas and Char, she'd be masturbating right in front of him, in the hopes of getting a little afternoon delight. It would be different if her sisters weren't both happily married. They thought sex with their husbands was something to be enjoyed no matter where or when they wanted it. They weren't animals, for God's sake. In their human form, it was best if they kept their activities confined to their homes, if not their bedrooms. Clarity thanked her lucky stars she had more control than they did.

"Let me see," Tom said, coming up behind her. "Maybe a fresh pair of eyes can spot the problem. How much are you off?"

"Seventeen hundred dollars," she replied, well aware that his eyes were glued to her breasts rather than the figures on the sheet lying on her desk. It was her own fault for wearing such a low cut, sheer blouse.

"Have you heard the latest from the office rumor mill?" Tom asked, his breath hot against her ear.

"Which one? The one that says the company is on the verge of bankruptcy or the one that says Daddy is dying of cancer and can't decide which one of us to leave the company to?"

"Neither," he said, shoving his hand down the front of her blouse. "This one says your whole family turns into werewolves at the full moon. Is that why you always have plans at that time of the month?" He fondled her breast and then tweaked her nipple.

Tom was too close to the truth to suit Clarity. "Where did you hear that line of bull? I've never turned into a wolf in my entire life. If you must know, I always avoid people at that time of the month because they use the full moon as an excuse to act like idiots. I'm sick and tired of it. I learned a long time ago it was a good night for me to curl up with a good book, a bowl of popcorn, and a glass of wine."

"If I'm a good boy and bring the wine, can we get together tomorrow night? I even have a hot DVD we can watch to get us in the mood."

Like I need something to get me in the mood. If I weren't at work, I'd be jumping his bones just for suggesting something like that. "If it will nip this ugly rumor in the bud, why not? I'll even pop for a tray of shrimp and make my special dip. Does this mean we're not still on for tonight? As I recall, you promised to take me to that new Japanese restaurant on the lake."

"Of course, we're going out tonight. I plan to pick up where we left off last night. I'm hot for you, honey, and don't you forget it."

Tom kissed her long and hard before he left her office, promising an exciting evening to come. Even though he hadn't helped her find the discrepancy, she had other things to think about. Somehow she had to stop the rumor that was circulating through the office like a wildfire in a drought. As far as she knew, no one other than her parents and sisters were aware of their Wolfen characteristics, and no one else in the clan ever mentioned them. Even though she was the youngest, she felt it her duty to protect Chas and Char as well as her father from these rumors. Hopefully, entertaining Tom tomorrow night would put an end to it. She certainly wouldn't be turning into a wolf, and that in itself should help.

It was just past one when Chas entered her office. "When are you going to get married, Clari? Justin is so good in bed I don't know how I got along without him all those years. Char and I have been talking, and we think you and Tom should—"

"We should what? Get married? I don't think I'm the marrying kind, like the two of you. Besides, why screw up good sex? You know I'm one hundred percent human. I can get my jollies with more than one guy. That's why I wouldn't be comfortable with just one man. It's too restricting."

Chas smiled. "You're my sister, and I love you dearly, but you don't know what you're talking about. The next blue moon is coming soon, and Daddy's got his heart set on another moonlight mating with you and Tom getting married then."

"You can't be serious. It's one thing for him to arrange your marriage to Justin and Char's to Lucas, but I'm not a Wolfen princess. The continuity of the family line does not rest as heavily on my shoulders as it does on yours. I'm just the number pusher around here."

"Like hell you are. You know you're a Blue Moon Princess, Wolfen or not. You know that Daddy depends on your premonitions, like the one you had about Lucas and Char being in trouble in Las Vegas, or the one about Justin and

Lash going into the Betas' lair to rescue Lucas. You also know that Rowan would do anything to harness your powers. Please let Daddy find you a husband, or at least talk to Tom about the two of you getting married. It would be better than all of us having to worry about the Betas doing harm to you because of your powers."

"Look, Chas, my powers are not common knowledge outside of the family. Unless someone close to me is spilling their guts to Rowan, I'm nothing more than the black sheep of the family, and you know how sheep and wolves get along."

Clarity no more than spoke the words when lights exploded behind her eyes. She knew the feeling all too well. A premonition was trying to materialize. From the severity of the pain in her head, she knew this one would not have anything to do with happily ever after.

*****

Tom left Clarity's office. He liked the way she got all flustered when he mentioned the werewolf rumor. Joanna and his mother were best friends as kids. It wasn't until Charles asked Joanna to find a husband for Clarity that his mother had heard from her one-time friend. Tom was like Clarity in more ways than she knew. His father was a silver beard like Charles, and an Elite to boot. His two older brothers had married well and were breeding up a storm. For him, it had been different. He, like Clarity, had no Wolfen characteristics. Instead, his humanity came with psychic powers. Even though his brothers considered him inferior, his premonitions had saved their sorry asses more than once.

He headed toward Charles Langford's office when the bright light of premonition assaulted his senses. Clari was in trouble. He knew it. He needed to talk to Charles.

He waited in the outer office until Cordelia told him he could go in to see Charles. The man looked as intimidating today as he had the first time they'd met three months ago when Tom first arrived at Langford and Langford. He couldn't help but wonder if it was just the man's personality, or if he was put off by the fact that Tom was purely human, even though he was of the Elite clan. Would he have preferred that his younger daughter marry someone like Justin or Lucas, even though such a match wouldn't be right for her?

"Something on your mind, Morrison?" Charles asked once the door closed behind him.

"It's Clarity, sir."

"What is it? Don't you like her?"

Tom laughed. "Like is a pretty lightweight word. There's not a man in the world that wouldn't like her. I'd say it's more like love. I couldn't be happier about this match my mother and your wife have arranged."

"Then you're ready for the Blue Moon Ceremony that's coming in a few weeks?"

"I am, but I don't think she is. There's a problem."

"Problem? What kind of a problem? Isn't she attracted to you sexually?"

Tom thought about the love games they played just hours earlier, to say nothing of what he had planned for not only tonight, but also for tomorrow night.

"We're good in that department."

"Then what the hell is it, Morrison? Don't beat around the bush. Spit it out. What's going on with my daughter?" Charles' face had turned red and the cords in his neck stuck out.

It was evident that he was losing control. If he wasn't careful, he could morph into a wolf without even knowing it. Tom wondered how he could explain what he didn't completely understand himself.

"Nothing yet, but you have to know of her psychic powers. Well, I have those same powers, and with them, I sense there is going to be trouble for her."

"What kind of trouble?"

"I'm not sure yet. I just left her office and got the beginnings of a premonition. It could take hours or even days for it to completely materialize. All I can tell you is that something is going to happen, and I'm worried about it."

Charles nodded. "I understand. I know that's how things happen with Clarity. Sometimes she never knows exactly what the visions mean. It certainly is unsettling, but I've learned to live with it. I guess I don't have to tell you that it's imperative you keep her safe. Will you be with her tonight?"

"Yes, and tomorrow night as well."

Charles raised an eyebrow. "She's agreed to go out on the night of the full moon? She usually lays low during that time. I think she's afraid of morphing like the rest of us, but of course we know that won't happen. She's like her mother in that respect. If I'm not mistaken, you're the same way. It's the curse of being the third child."

Tom would have never called it a curse. For him, it was more like a blessing. His brothers both needed to morph whenever they had sex. He thanked his lucky stars he didn't have to endure anything like that just to get laid. If the truth were known, he liked the fact he had the instincts of being Elite but none of the drawbacks. His only affliction was those damnable visions.

"Call it what you want, Charles, but I'm very happy with my position in the clan, as I think is Clarity. We aren't going out tomorrow night. She's allowing me to come over and watch a DVD with her while we enjoy a glass of good wine. I'm bringing the wine and the DVD, and she's supplying not only the apartment, but also the shrimp. If I have my way, the shrimp will only be the appetizer."

"Are you telling me you plan to take her sexually?"

"I'm discreet enough not to kiss and tell. She's not like her sisters, Charles. Unless I miss my guess, she's been sexually active for a long time. It's best that way. I never did get excited about being the first one with a virgin."

Charles' face turned red with embarrassment at Tom's blunt description of his youngest daughter. The man wasn't used to dealing with the human aspect of the Elite clan. It was common knowledge that human Elites were no different than any other human when it came to sexuality. While their Wolfen sisters didn't come into heat until after their thirtieth birthday, human Elites experimented far earlier and were much more experienced.

Dear Reader,

I hope you enjoyed **Twice In A Blue Moon**. I have to tell you, I really love the characters of Charity and Lucas. Many readers wrote me asking: "What's next for them? What about their friends Bran, Garth, or even Valerie? What about Kill, will he strike back?" Well, stay tuned as my Blue Moon world continues. They'll all be back in *Stealing a Blue Moon Princess*. Will there find be a happy ending? Wait and see.

When I wrote **Twice In a Blue Moon** , I got so many letters from fans thanking me for the book. As an author, I love feedback. Frankly, you are the reason that I write. So, tell me what you liked, what you loved, even what you hated. I'd love to hear from you. You can write me at atasteofhoneyjans@gmail.com and visit me on the web at http://honeyjanserotica.blogspot.com/

Finally, I need to ask a favor, if you're so inclined, I'd love a review of **Twice In A Blue Moon**. Loved it, hated it, whatever you really think—I'd just enjoy your feedback.

As you might know, reviews can be tough to come by these days. You, the reader, have the power now to make or break a book, or an author. If you have the time, here's a link to my author page on Amazon. You can find all of my books here— http://www.amazon.com/Honey-Jans/e/B007OWPNHW/

Thank you so much for reading, and for spending time with me.

In gratitude,

Honey Jans

www.ingramcontent.com/pod-product-compliance
Lightning Source LLC
Chambersburg PA
CBHW070508130626
46555CB00003B/1213